To Thank you for being you!

SPRING TRAINING MURDERS

By

Roland Hopkins

Branden Books, Boston

Love Daddy

© Copyright 2013
By Branden Books

Library of Congress Cataloging-in-Publication Data

Hopkins, Roland.
　Spring Training Murders / by Roland Hopkins.
　　pages cm
ISBN 978-0-8283-2496-0 (pbk. : alk. paper) -- ISBN 978-0-8283-2497-7 (e-book)
1. Private investigators--Massachusetts--Boston--Fiction.
2. Mystery fiction.
3. Baseball stories. I. Title.

PS3558.O6363S68 2013
813'.54--dc23

　　　　　　2013030106

Paperback: ISBN 9780828324960
E-Book ISBN 9780828324977

Roland Hopkins is also the author of *Snowball in Hell* now also available in Paperback and E-Book editions.

Branden Books
PO Box 812094
Wellesley MA 02482

www.brandenbooks.com

SYNOPSIS

SPRING TRAINING MURDERS brings the reader back to simpler times right after World War Two when the Boston Red Sox were breaking their humps to beat the Damn Yankees for the pennant and World Series. But that all takes an explosive back seat when a rookie pitching phenom falls fowl, disappears, and shows up murdered. The first place home team needs no bad publicity, so the exasperated owner hires a local, hard-boiled PI Jonathan Dark to suit up and pass himself off as a professional ballplayer. Packed with nonstop drama and richly drawn authentic characters, the action thriller hits a home run as the unpredictable plot thickens to include a captivating love story, a violent kidnapping, much mafia mayhem, and a hit man assassination. Whodunit? The rapid page-turner leads in many directions holding the reader often breathless and in suspense right up 'till the games' over.

PROLOGUE

2012 CELEBRATES THE 100TH YEAR ANNIVERSARY OF FENWAY PARK, major league baseball's most famous ballpark. On a warm afternoon, April 20th, over 250 former players gathered at the famous old but completely remodeled stadium. Red Sox Hall of Famers Carl Yastremski, Carlton Fisk, Jim Rice, Wade Boggs, and many others thrilled the over thirty-eight thousand fans who attended for the memories. Very few players represented the Pennant winning 1946 team for obvious reasons, and when the lovable old shortstop, 92-year-old Johnny Pesky was asked about the authenticity of actions depicted in this not-yet-written book, he frowned, and then denied the events ever occurred. Hall of Fame second baseman 94-year-old Bobby Doerr was also in attendance and refused to answer any questions put to him by me, the soon—to-be author. Doerr only smiled.

The ninety-two year old ex-private detective featured in this book, who also had one at bat for the team in 1946, quietly attended the celebration, was not recognized or interviewed by anyone other than yours truly, thus leaving the truth or fiction of this tale to you, the reader. When you finish reading you are invited to contact any one of the many Boston sports reporters with your findings. Tweet, Linked in, Face book - and maybe the truth will finally be revealed. Or not!

I have known Mr. Dark, a former private detective, for many years. Back in the day we shared a restaurant table at Suffolk Downs at least once a week. Most race trackers don't make money gambling, but they dream of breaking even, and utterly enjoy the most exciting two minutes in sports when they feel the tingle run up and down their spine as the thousand pound nags hit the top of the stretch and race toward the finish wire – the final furlong.

In the eighties I owned a few of those cheap nags as a hobby and visited Suffering Downs at least twice a week to see if I could get my picture taken in the Winner's Circle – always an owner's dream. That's where I ran into Mr. Dark who was then a former private detective, an avid Red Sox fan, and also a thoroughbred fan. He spun a lot of interesting tales of his exciting P.I. past, meeting and sharing drinks with famous people like Babe Ruth, John Wayne, and a young Harvard student named Jack Kennedy. I sat on every word and believed half his tales. Besides, he was a pretty decent handicapper, and occasionally we'd go home winners, especially if one of my cheapies won. In the early nineties I sold my few nags, retired, and moved away from Beantown, losing all contact with my P.I. pal.

I was totally shocked to recognize him sitting in the grandstand on that warm April 20, 2012 Fenway Park celebration day - hunched over, thin, wrinkled and bald. He still vaguely resembled the forties and fifties movie idol Alan Ladd - just a very old version. At first I hesitated as I did the math. He had to be in his nineties, and he always claimed to have had one at bat with the Red Sox in 1946, but never pushed the story. So no one ever checked or disputed him. Everyone knew he had been a star in the Boston Park League in the forties, fifties and sixties. But a major leaguer?

So I grabbed the seat beside him and gave him a soft hug that he returned very delicately. He recognized me and said, "Hey kid, got an hour to hear an interesting story? I decided that I gotta tell it before I croak. And when you hear it you'll know why I never told it before."

I hugged the elderly man again and nodded.

"I'm ninety-two years old," he began. "And I always promised myself to take this story to the grave with me. But lately I've been wondering why the hell the Lord allows me to be around so long. That's what happens when you age. You'll see, but ---. He hesitated as he perused my pretty well preserved seventy-six year form. "You got a few more years to waste, kid. But me? Maybe I lasted this long so the story could be told. Probably my worst screw-up, but hey, you be the judge."

I gazed out over the green grassy field covered now with the many ballplayers who had been invited to attend the 100th anniversary. Being a writer I always carried a small notebook and tape recorder just in case. Hey, maybe this was the case, so I said: "Start talking, Mr. Dark. I'm all ears."

And here's the murder and mayhem story he told me on that warm celebration day at the famous 100-year old Fenway Park – and I will do my best to repeat the tale in his words.

BOSTON POST HEADLINES   1946

PRESIDENT TRUMAN ENDS ALL RATIONING

IT'S A WONDERFUL LIFE STARRING JAMES STEWART NOMINATED FOR ACADEMY AWARD

BILL VEECK BUYS CLEVELAND INDIANS FOR $2.2 MILLION

MEMO, appearing in the Boston Red Sox locker room, August 23, 1946:

To all ballplayers and other team personal: Stephen Majors, a spring training attendee is no longer affiliated with this ball club. And, for the best interests of everyone concerned, no one knows or has ever had any contact with this gentleman.

Signed, Thomas A. Yawkey, owner

CHAPTER ONE

BOSTON POST HEADLINES 1946

US ATOMIC ENERGY COMMISSION ESTABLISHED

US POPULATION REPORTED AT 141,388,566

"**WHAT THE HELL ARE YOU DOIN' MAN?** I ain't ever done nuthin' to you."

The victim was tall, lean, handsome and young. The perp was bigger, wider, and wore a black stocking cap over his face. "Shudup asshole," the man whispered as though someone might overhear.

It was a dusky midnight at the Charlestown Navy Yard, pretty much deserted since the end of World War 2. The captor had stolen a Boston taxi cab earlier in the evening, followed the intended victim to an upscale Commonwealth Avenue apartment building, patiently waited, and picked up the unsuspecting guy as he was exiting the building close to midnight.

"Where to, Mack?" the pseudo cabby had mumbled.

The victim had answered in a stumbling mutter, almost unintelligible like he had either been drinking, smoking, sniffing, or just half asleep. The perp knew his victim's addictions. "The K – Kenmore Hotel. I – I'm gonna be famous."

The driver chuckled under his breath. "Not for the reason you think, asshole," he whispered.

"Wha - what was that you said?" the passenger asked, and then paused, staring through blurred eyes at the cabby's picture framed on the back of the front seat. "Hey man, this ain't you in this photo. Where'd you get this cab?"

"The regular driver is sick. Don't worry. We're almost home for you. Close your eyes and take a nap."

The victim took the advice and closed his eyes.

Twenty minutes later he was awakened and found himself facing a pistol held by the now stocking masked cab driver.

"Make no noise and get outta the cab," the soon-to-be executor said. "And head for those wooden dock stairs over there. We're goin' to the beach."

They were parked in front of a long deserted wharf.

The victim, scared shitless, obeyed without further encouragement. At the bottom of the stairs he noticed a two-foot cardboard box filled with what looked like soft cement. He had read about gangster killings using what's called Cement Shoes and then throwing the target into the water to drown. His head started to pound. He didn't understand who this guy was or why he was being attacked. *One of my fuckin' jealous teammates musta got real pissed off at me,* he pondered. *I wonder which one.*

"Take your shoes off and step into that box," the captor ordered.

The victim hesitated, but quickly realized the futility of stalling when he felt his midsection being squeezed tightly and heard and felt his ribs cracking.

The man gruffly said, "I can kill ya now, or give ya a fightin' chance. And if you're smart enough to know anything about the ocean, you're aware of the twelve-hour tides. Six hours in and six hours out."

Thoughts suddenly flooded the captive's aching head of when his teacher would take him fishing and point out the best times to catch – incoming tides the best - outgoing the worst.

He strained his neck to check which way the few boats were facing.

"Don't waist your eyes," the masked man barked. "The tide's dead low right now and starting to return. I'm gonna tie ya to this wharf-post right here. The new tide will eventually cover it up to the dock. That's about two feet above your head. So ya got about five hours to figure out how to get loose. You can yell and scream. But I don't think no one's gonna hear ya. Sorry! This place has become a ghost town since the end of the war. Too bad! If I was a real estate developer I'd buy it and build apartments."

The captive went silent and obeyed, realizing that his only chance was to as quickly as possible get the death sentence show on the road and the killer as far away as possible. So he forced his feet into the squishy, still soft cement. Then he was pushed up against the post and rope-tied - his hands behind his back and the post. His now cemented feet were buried beneath the sand, making it even more difficult to get free.

The captor, his face still covered with the black stocking mask, chuckling said," Okay Mr. Majors, let's see you pitch yourself outta this game. And I don't think your swimming ability will help you here."

Majors managed to get the last words in as he watched the man climb back onto the wharf and disappear from view. "Fuck you," he yelled at the top of his lungs. "I'll get outta here and fucking find you."

CHAPTER TWO
BOSTON POST HEADLINES 1946

FIRST AUTOMATIC ELECTRICAL DIGITAL COMPUTER DEDICATED AT PENN. UNIV.

HOLLYWOOD'S W.C. FIELDS DIES AT 66

MY NAME IS JONATHAN DARK. My friends call me Johnny. I'm a young, hardboiled private eye like Sam Spade or Philip Marlowe. *I wish!* They're movie, radio, and book heroes - follow the script and never lose. I'm small time, make a few bucks, work a lot of divorces, missing person cases that usually turn out to be people who want to be missing, and also handle some non-essential stuff that the cops give up on. I'm a frustrated weekend Park League baseball player who has had two tryouts with the Boston Red Sox, both times hitting the shit out of the ball and twisting a faulty knee. If you're a ball fan I think you'll like this white-knuckle ride of missed opportunity and whodunit stuff. In retrospect I think I enjoyed most of it, fell in love, and even got paid for a lot of my efforts.

Is my story true?

No one has yet proved it otherwise. And only two of the players along with myself are left from the 1946 pennant winning team – and we all agreed sixty-six years ago to not spill the beans.

So fasten your seatbelt and I'll take you on a sport's filled whodunit season with the 1946 World Series Boston Red Sox.

CHAPTER THREE

BOSTON POST HEADLINES 1946

12 NAZI LEADERS SENTENCED TO HANG AT NUREMBERG TRIALS

LOST WEEKEND WINS ACADEMY AWARD FOR BEST PICTURE

I HAD BEEN SUMMONED TO RED SOX OWNER Tom Yawkey's expensively furnished office located in Boston's Fenway Park overlooking the ball field. The millionaire was born 1903 in Detroit to immense wealth. The sports writers labeled him a financier and gentleman sportsman. He preferred to hunt, fish, and follow his baseball team rather than manage his fortune. The nephew and later adopted son of Bill Yawkey, once owner of the Detroit Tigers, Tom inherited over 43 million dollars from his uncle. Needless to say, even in the deepest Depression years he was never in want for ready cash. And he never forgot what his uncle had told him almost too many times. "It isn't the hand you're dealt, my boy, it's how you play it. And you were dealt five aces - so don't screw it up."

Mr. Yawkey spent mucho dollars buying established ballplayers attempting to live up to his uncle's challenge. He wanted to win a World Series.

The Red Sox owner motioned for me to sit on a comfortable appearing easy chair featuring thick, cushioned arms. The wide window behind the rich man's paper-cluttered desk brightly framed late-morning Fenway Park where the famous Babe Ruth had begun his career 32 years earlier. The far wall was decorated with three large framed pictures, maybe four feet wide by six feet high. One was a young teenage Babe Ruth, six feet two inches tall and 215 strong pounds of weight. He was dressed in a droopy Red Sox uniform. 1914! Nineteen years old! A pitcher! Who knew? The middle pic showed a musclebound Jimmy Foxx, 6 feet in height and 195 in weight with muscles that could rival any heavyweight boxer. He had actually rivaled the Babe as a hitter, slugging 58 homers in 1932. When he joined the Sox he smacked 50 in 1938. The third giant portrait showed a skinny Ted Williams, the currant superstar and easily a rival to Ruth and Foxx. He was just getting started. Mr. Yawkey had spent millions since buying the team in 1933 and come up empty every year. "Those damn Yankees keep beating me," he grumbled. "Screw the Yankees. They always have one more good pitcher. But this is my year, kid. Hey, Teddy boy is almost as good as the Babe. Don't you think?"

I felt a bit uncomfortable, a feeling I always experienced when in the presence of wealthy, white-collar snobs. Williams had batted a phenomenal .406 in 1941, and then had another great season in 1942, and then was drafted into the Air Force - serving 4 years defending our country.

"Didn't you get a tryout here last year?" Mr. Yawkey asked and coughed on his own smelly, expensive cigar smoke that floated to the white ceiling. "My manager says you could hit pretty good. But you twisted a knee – or something. Right?"

The manager was Joe Cronin, a former all-star shortstop of the Washington Senators. Years earlier he had married the daughter of the Washington team's owner. But that's another story for another day.

I flipped my gray fedora with snap brimmed lid onto an adjoining chair and fired up a Chesterfield. I used a wooden match with my thumbnail to light it, and then broke the match in two and placed it in a standup ashtray. Pals occasionally teased me for my stark resemblance to movie star idol Alan Ladd. I was at least a foot taller and sported an unruly head of dark hair as opposed to Ladd's attractive blonde looks that fascinated the females along with some fairy males. Ladd's fame stemmed from his cute face, but also a very masculine deep voice. I debated growing a bushy beard, but never did. It didn't hurt being compared to Hollywood's number one heartthrob.

Mr. Yawkey said, "Joe says that you're a twenty-six year old local shamus looking for work. And you got a reputation of being able to keep your mouth shut – sort of like lawyer/client, or doctor/patient privilege."

"That sums me up pretty well," I said. I was wearing my only 3-piece gray flannel suit that was wrinkled and looked cheap. My tight knitted black necktie was frayed - but the only one I owned. Mr. Yawkey wore three pieces - all silk - or appeared to be silk, and a clean silk hanky in the top jacket pocket. He had my attention and continued. "My secretary checked you out yesterday. Says that you're cleanly shaven and some of the local single females were known to have giggled behind your back whispering that if you had blonde hair you'd resemble movie idol Alan Ladd."

A backward compliment, I thought. *I'd really rather resemble Humphrey Bogart.* I took a deep drag and blew a large smoke ring, and then watched it float toward the ceiling. I then puffed a smaller one right through it. "I'm six feet-two and proud of it."

"Hey, that's pretty clever," the team owner said referring to the smoke ring. "Can you teach me?"

I chuckled. "The dames love it. Always gets an encore. Sometimes more! Yeah, I can teach you, but that isn't why you got me up here. If you need an investigator I'm sure as shootin' that you can afford the best. Pinkerton has the top reputation in the business."

A suddenly serious look masked Mr. Yawkey's face. The slightly overweight chubby bodied middle-aged man wore a crew cut - not common on millionaires. "You knew Buck Jones, the cowboy movie star?"

I felt puzzled at the change of tone. "Jones was my favorite – better then Gene Autry and Roy Rodgers. Why? How did you know I knew him? And what difference does it make?"

The owner smiled and blew a cigar smoke ring shaped like an egg. "I looked into your background, son. You were in the Coconut Grove nightclub that horrible November night in 1942 when it burned down. Right?"

I hesitated, unfolded and refolded my arms and then nodded. "I try and forget that event, if you don't mind."

"Buck Jones died that night being just like the hero he portrayed on the silver screen," the team owner said. "I understand he kept running back into the burning building bringing out survivors."

I slowly nodded.

"And you were right beside him?"

I nodded again. "Buck ran in one last time. I didn't!"

"And he died – you didn't," Mr. Yawkey added, and then wiped a small tear from his eye. "I lost a close friend in that fire."

"Over four hundred died that night. I think the fire code allowed for a capacity of about three hundred. Something wrong with that picture! The popular joint was always filled with more than three hundred."

"Is it true that the owner had locked the fire doors from the outside so people couldn't sneak out without paying their checks?"

I went silent. I wasn't enjoying the ugly reminiscing. "Someone did," I finally answered. "Buck and I tried to force two of them open. No dice!"

"And people panicked and got squashed in the revolving doors?"

"It was a mess. Those doors are for looks – not easy to use for escaping."

"But something good came out of it," the team owner said. "The city has changed a lot of its fire codes as a result. No more revolving doors as the sole entrance and exit."

I didn't answer hoping to get off the subject, but I had always thought that they could have changed all the codes before and saved a lot of innocent lives. "So that's why you want to hire me - because I saved a few people from dying in a fire? Anyone would have done what I did."

"I don't think so. But you were even a bigger hero by not hanging around to get medals. I respect people like you. Your Uncle Bill told Joe Cronin that afterwards you just went home, showered, and went to bed."

I tried not to blush. *Tough shamuses don't blush,* I told myself.

The owner relit his thick, smelly cigar - blew another egg-shaped ring and watched it flout to the ceiling and then break up. "I'll practice smoke rings later. Right now I have a big problem with my team. I'm hoping you can help me solve a sticky situation without any unnecessary publicity. Join the squad!"

I suddenly felt both knees turn to rubber. *Could this rich fool actually want me to play?* I asked myself as I laced my fingers on my lap and sat upright. "I've already had two tryouts with your team, sir. Both times my knee gave way. I can hit, though. And throw? No one throws better. Just can't run."

"Not to play, son," the owner said putting his hand out like a traffic cop. "I don't need a player. I need a private detective who can pass for a ballplayer. Undercover stuff."

Now I really feel like a jerk, I told myself. *But if he wants me to put out a fire, hell - that's what I get paid for.*

Mr. Yawkey, enthroned in his large, posh, leather office chair, nodded with a wide smile, and then reached into his teak desk drawer and removed a snifter of brandy. He loved to mingle with his players. Many a summer evening he would stay until dusk taking batting practice. His ambition was to hit the 60-foot tall, green left field wall - nicknamed THE GREEN MONSTER. Afterwards, he'd hang with a few drinkers and pick up the tabs. He liked the drinkers, and the drinkers liked him.

"Drink?" he offered. "The sun is over the yardarm somewhere in the world."

A fashionable grandfather clock standing in a dusky corner read noon. "I try to hold off 'till after work hours," I lied, my observant eyes circuiting the opulent room, stopping at the three large fames holding maybe three of the greatest hitters of all time. My *Uncle Bill used to drink with the Babe,* I recalled to myself.

Mr. Yawkey twisted off the top of the bottle and swigged half. "Sure you won't join me?"

I succumbed to the temptation, took the liquid and finished it. I coughed and reiterated, "I can hit and throw, sir. I just can't run."

The owner shook his head. "No calling me sir, my boy. Call me Tom. I'm just an old fool who loves the sport and inherited a lot of dough. J. Paul Getty wisely gave a tip on getting rich: 'Early to bed, early to rise, and inherit a fortune.' That's what happened to me. Only I go to bed late and sleep late." He smiled, shrugged his shoulders, and puffed on his stogie. "I guess that's almost the same thing. Same result anyway! I'm going to win a World Series here, or die trying."

"May I ask why you need a private eye?"

The boss leaned forward, cupped his hands over his mouth, and whispered, "Murder! I think one of my ballplayers murdered another one of my ballplayers."

My eyes widened as I rubbed my chin in thought. "I follow the team pretty closely, sir. I mean Tom. You're fifteen games in first place. Dave Ferris has already won twenty. I don't recall any killings reported lately. Is someone missing that the public doesn't know about?"

"Majors! A rookie kid! Steve Majors."

I pondered the information, and then nodded. "Yeah, I read about him during Spring Training. Then he just kinda disappeared and I thought I read in the Post sport's page that he returned to the team last week and was supposed to pitch tomorrow."

The Red Sox owner grabbed another snifter from his desk and began to sip.

I removed my small notebook from my jacket pocket. "When did Majors go missing, and have you called the police yet?"

The owner shook his head. "I can't afford the publicity. Got a reputation to protect. My ballplayers aren't supposed to go around breaking the law - especially murder."

I moved my fingers over my mouth. "No problem! I can keep secrets. Zip your lip and save a ship."

Mr. Yawkey snuffed out the stogie he was smoking, removed a new cigar from a gold box, licked it, snipped off the end with a shiny nail clipper, and then lit it with a gold cigarette lighter. "Join me?" he asked, raising his eyebrows.

I crinkled my nose. "Can't stand the smell. But you go ahead. I'll suffer."

The owner hesitated for a long moment, puffed, and then stared into my eyes. "Majors pitched in an industrial league last year and struck out 27 batters in one game. Quite a feat in any league! We inked the kid and brought him to Spring Training. Cost us five hundred."

"Sounds like a swell move to me. Seems that I read that he was a whiz in Spring Training."

"He looked great. Another Bob Feller with a fastball clocked at close to 100 miles per hour. And he did fine until he got stopped for drunken driving. The kid is a phenom."

Mr. Yawkey flipped the switch on a small radio that was playing an Academy Award tune by Hoagy Carmichael - Ole

Buttermilk Sky. The owner hummed a few bars and let out a long sigh. "The kid smokes dope. He's hooked! Opium! Reefers! Everything! Anything! When he's sober he's charming, but very conceited. His movie star looks grab the gals. Another reason he would have been a drawing card for the fans. He was definitely going to make the difference this year. I hired a personal shrink for him to privately rehab. They secretly stayed in Florida until two weeks ago, and then we flew the kid in and activated him. You're right. He was going to pitch tomorrow."

"You guys did a good job keeping his addiction a secret. So what happened?"

"I stay on the good side of the press. Cost me a few pennies and tickets, but it's worth it. I don't need any scandals."

"I mean, what happened to Majors?"

The concerned owner took a deep drag on his cigar. "Most people only have to wrestle with one demon. Mine is alcohol. I know it and try to keep it in check. But this poor kid has two demons - drugs and his cock. He loves women. He even propositioned Jean - my wife."

I lapsed into a thoughtful silence, scribbled a few more notes, and finally interjected, "And you think he was caught with his cock in the wrong hole?"

Mr. Yawkey flinched. "Maybe! During Spring Training two of the players nailed him red-handed. One of them almost beat the kid to death. The other one just threatened to kill him. I can't have that kind of behavior around here. So I roomed him with Rudy York. Rudy's big, tough, and is single. Doesn't even date as far as I know. I even agreed to pay Rudy a few extra dollars to be the kid's bodyguard."

"Wrong bodyguard?"

"Rudy drinks too. Too much, I guess. The night Majors disappeared I'm pretty sure that Rudy was drunk. Yeah, I guess I picked the wrong man for the job. But all the other players hated Majors."

The team owner removed a snapshot from his desk and handed it to me. "This is Majors."

I studied the small photo, turning it sideways, even upside down. "Yeah, you're right. Cute! He looks like Errol Flynn. And we all know his reputation with the dames. In like Flynn!"

"Would have been great for attendance," Mr. Yawkey nodded and said. "Winning the World Series with him was my goal. I spent a lot of money to build this ball club. And I think you're right. Majors might've slept with the wrong woman - or got in with the wrong crowd trying to feed his dope habit. Those mugs are dangerous."

"You said he was conceited and the other players didn't like him?"

"Yes siree! He was an arrogant, know-it-all asshole. Bragged about his conquests to anyone who'd listen. By the way, do you carry a gun?"

I shook my head. "I own one and have a license, but I must admit that private-eye work isn't anything like you read in the Chandler and Hammett stories in Black Mask Magazine, or hear on the radio. Hey, Alan Ladd has a new detective show on the squawk box. It's called BOX 13. Have you heard it?"

Mr. Yawkey rubbed his hands together. "Every week. It's on the same station that carries my games."

"Well, I'm awfully sorry to break your balloon, but most of my cases are boring divorce stuff, or insurance frauds. Spent two years as a cop, but I've never needed a gun yet in this racket."

Mr. Yawkey leaned back in his chair and again sized me up in obvious anticipation of hiring me. "You must've learned the art of self defense in the police force. I'm sure that occasion could come up at any time in your line of work."

I leaned forward and removed a simple ink pen from Mr. Yawkey's ink well. I then glanced around the room a few times, finally zeroing in on the wood paneling around the door that led to the outer office. "Watch," I said, raised my right arm and flipped the ink pen across the room, maybe fifteen feet. It stuck, point first into the wooden panel about waist high. "That would stun most attackers for a moment," I said, chuckling.

"Used that talent more than once. I can also throw a guy out at the plate from dead center field in the air."

Mr. Yawkey's eyes seemed to pop. He leaned forward over his desk and asked, "How the hell did you learn that talent? The ink pen, not the smoke rings."

"My uncle taught me. He's been in a wheelchair since the end of World War One and he loves sports. So he took up darts and made a bundle in barrooms. Hey, everyone's good at something. Ya know?"

Mr. Yawkey pressed a button on top of his desk. The door to his office immediately opened. A young, pretty, well-dressed, and nicely figured brunette entered carrying a notebook and pen. "Yes Mr. Yawkey, can I help?"

Her name was Penny Michaels. A local girl born in 1925, she grew up in the middle to lower class Revere Beach area, just across the Mystic River from the big city - Boston. An "A" student in high school, she won a scholarship to the exclusive Katie Gibbs secretarial school and learned top-notch typing, short hand - along with accounting skills. Despite of her young age, Mr. Yawkey deemed her a valuable piece in his baseball puzzle. She kept the office organized, was single, an almost perfect lady, an unconscious flirt, and engaged. How did I know that? One thing Private Eyes do before visiting projected clients is their homework and find out as much as possible about the people involved. Celebrities are easy. Before my visit I knew all about Tom Yawkey, Ted Williams, and a few other ballplayers. I have a pal at the Boston Post newspaper. When dealing with less famous people like Penny, the search becomes more difficult. You have to discover someone who knows them personally. Seek and ye shall find – or something like that. I did attend Sunday School way back when. So I sought information on Mr. Yawkey's secretary and found out lots from a girl who went to school with her. After a few extra drinks at a local barroom she gave me the bio. *Bully for me!* The girl was quite cute and we ---. Well, that's a story for another day.

"This is Mr. Dark, Penny," Mr. Yawkey introduced. "He's going to join the club as a pinch hitter. Can you draw him a check for five hundred, please?"

I abruptly stood up, reached out a soft hand and shook. "I'm Johnny Dark. How do you like me so far?" I had always wanted to use that line, never had before, and now waited to see how it worked. I could feel her bright blue eyes perusing my six-foot plus figure - head to toe as she fluttered her eyelashes, tilted her head, half smiled, let go of my hand, and turned to leave the room. I knew she resembled a hot movie star. Jean Tierney? Yeah! I had just seen the popular movie LAURA starring Dana Andrews, Clifton Webb, and Jean who had given me a slight, but embarrassing boner forcing me to keep the popcorn box over my lap during the entire show.

Penny stopped and double-taked as she noticed the fountain pen sticking in the doorframe. She threw a questioning glance at her boss who just grinned, tilted his head towards me, and shrugged. She mimicked the shrug and left the room. I felt as though maybe she had been mentally undressing me. *That's okay for us guys to do,* I reminded myself, *but ---?* In less than 30 seconds she returned, sashayed across the room and sat in a straight-backed wooden chair beside the boss's desk. I returned the Superman x-ray eye trick, imagining a burlesque show-stopping figure under her loose silk blouse and too-long quilted skirt. *Damn, she looks just like Gene Tierney,* I thought. *Long, wavy black hair, swell figure, and pert lips – very kissable.*

Penny opened a large, hard covered brown leather-bound checkbook and began writing. **Jonathan Dark. 500 dollars.** She looked up and smiled. "That's a nice bonus for an unknown. Five thousand a year is base salary for other rookies and this year is almost over."

I began biting a cuticle, looked at the ceiling, and then out of the office window anticipating batting practice on the Fenway ball field - a dream of every little tyke who grew up in the area. *How many dreams ever come true other than Dorothy Gale when she clicks her heals together at the end of the Wizard of Oz movie and says, there's no place like home?*

Penny daintily arose and handed me the check. "Welcome aboard, Johnny. Maybe we'll see each other again." She smiled at her boss and left the room, swaying her butt as she closed the door.

I got up to leave, grabbed my hat, and then turned to my new boss. "I always wanted two things in life, Mr. Yawkey, I mean Tom - both of them seeming very elusive. Fighting in the war for my country was the first, and playing Major League baseball was the second. Or the other way around! Looks like I'll reach one of them. I'll be able to tell my kids that I was on the same team with Ted Williams, Bobby Doerr, Johnny Pesky, Rudy York, Dave Ferris and Dom DiMaggio - a bunch of All-Stars."

The team owner shot a fleeting look across his desk. "And one of them may be a murderer," he coughed. "Check in with Johnny Orlando our equipment manager. He'll issue you a uniform. Care about a number?"

I chuckled. "One?"

"Sorry, that's Bobby Doerr."

"How about Nine?"

"I don't think Ted would ever speak to me again, or you either."

"I'm just kidding, Tom. I don't care what number I have. You're hiring me to do a job. Any hints?"

"You'll stay at the Kenmore Hotel and room with Rudy. As I told you, York was rooming with Majors before the rook disappeared exactly one week ago. Rudy was a great slugger, and is sadly now at the end of his career. And yeah, he's a heavy drinker. Maybe you can help me there, too. Try and keep his drinking to a bare minimum." He rubbed his chin. "Yesiree, I'll tell you what. If Rudy drives in a hundred runs this season, there's a bonus in it for you. And I never trusted a man who didn't take a few drinks. Two of baseball's greatest drinkers were also the greatest home run hitters. I've shared several highballs with Babe Ruth and Hack Wilson. Ruth holds the American League record of 60 homers, and Hack the National League with 56. I often wondered how many times those two slugged one out of the park with a lousy hangover."

"I'll do my best to unravel the mystery - and I'll also take care of Rudy," I said, getting up to leave.

"By the way, besides a fountain pen, do you carry any other kind of weapon?"

I lifted my leg like movie star dog Lassie, pulled up my pant leg that revealed a thin nine-inch knife attached a small belt that held up my socks. "No one sees this. But it comes in handy to open my overdue bills."

Mr. Yawkey laughed. "I'm sure it does, and I hope you don't have to use it on this case."

I glanced down at the check I'd been given to by the boss's glamorous secretary. $500. I turned it over before pocketing it. The blouse had written something on the back of the check. **PENNY MITCHELL. HIghland 4-3804.** My heart skipped two beats. I smiled and bowed to my new boss, grabbed my hat and let myself out into the waiting room. *Maybe my new pick-up line worked.*

Penny Michaels was nowhere in sight.

CHAPTER FOUR

BOSTON POST HEADLINES 1946

UNITED NATIONS HOLDS FIRST MEETING

GALLON OF GAS RAISED TO 15 CENTS

I FELT LIKE AN EXUBERANT KID, overly excited that I was going to be a real live Red Sox player, or a pretend player. And more elated that I was going to be rooming with a real major leaguer - Rudy York.

The team owner had given me a neatly printed notebook describing the bios of each player, coaches, and the manager. These were the suspects of what? No one yet knew. I scanned York's bio. Six feet one inch tall, 200 pounds, 75% Indian. Came to the league in Detroit as a first baseman, but had to play behind one of baseball's greatest hitters - Hank Greenburg who hit 58 homers in 1938, just 2 from trying Babe Ruth's record. So Rudy never really got a full chance to display his baseball prowess until the war years when Hank was the first player to enlist and York was deemed 4F. In 1943 he led the American league in home runs and runs batted in. He was selected to the All-Star team five years in a row. In 1946, the Tigers, who got the five year older Greenburg back from the service, made the thirty-three year old York, who hadn't aged gracefully, available and traded him to Boston.

Harmless old fart, I thought as I parked my 1940 Plymouth Coupe with rumble seat across the street from the Kenmore Hotel in bustling Kenmore Square. Trolley cars and busses dropped fans off there every game-day afternoon and they then walked two short blocks to the park. Today's game was late afternoon. The Sox were to play against the lowly St. Louis Browns at four o'clock. I rode the elevator to the second floor, walked down a long hallway and found room 202. I lightly knocked. No answer! I tried the key that Mr. Yawkey had given me. It worked and the door slowly opened. A large figure of a man lay face down on one of the two single beds. A half empty scotch bottle standing on the bedside table next to him revealed what I didn't need to be a shamus to detect. The tobacco/alcohol/perspiration odor almost made me lose my breakfast. I opened both windows as wide as possible, flushed a dirty toilet bowl, and lit a Chesterfield. The big form stirred slowly, opened his eyes and squinted. The only Indians I had ever encountered were in the movies fighting the cowboys. York resembled all of them.

"You wanna rob me?" York coughed and reached for his scotch bottle.

I moved swiftly and grabbed it away. "Sorry, Mr. York. I'm your new roomy, Johnny Dark. Mr. Yawkey wants me to see if I can help you get to the ballpark on time."

Rudy cracked a yellow-toothed smile. "He wants you to watch my drinking?"

I noticed several burnt-down-to-almost-nothing cigarette butts in a full ashtray. "Not really! He wants me to make sure you don't get killed in a cigarette fire started by you."

The tired ballplayer grinned widely, pulled on his brown corduroy pants, walked to the hotel-room sink and rinsed his face with cold water. "I know I'm an alchy. It's ruined what coulda been a Hall of Fame career."

I placed my small suitcase on the floor in front of a closet. "I looked up your statistics. Mr. Yawkey said you're one of the reasons the team is in first place. He likes you."

Rudy lay back down on his bed and stared at the ceiling. "He's as much of an alchy as me. Nice man though! Sometimes I stay in the evening and throw batting practice to him. We share a fifth and he tries to hit the left field wall. You can join us sometime. He's a fun owner."

I looked around the room for a clock. "Got the time? The equipment manager told me to be at the park by three."

Rudy opened the bedside drawer and removed a silver pocket watch. "It's a little past noon. We got time for lunch and a few dimies. I'll buy! Game?"

"For lunch yes, but I'll pass on the beers. They may need me to pinch hit."

Rudy showered and shaved, put on a wrinkled, light colored summer suit and followed me into the hotel dining room.

"I spent five long years in the minors," Rudy said as he checked the lunch menu. "How about you?"

I debated a lie – and then decided to tell a partial truth. "I had a tryout in '41. Hit and fielded good, but cracked my knee that day rounding second. Kept me outta the Army. 4F, you know. It just never healed correctly. Had a tryout again last year. I figured if one-armed Pete Gray could play during the war years for St. Louis, maybe a one legged guy could make some team."

Everyone knew the one-armed Pete Grey story and York nodded. He'd played against the phenom and watched him catch a fly ball, flip the ball in the air, drop his glove, catch the ball again and throw it to the infield.

I finished telling my new roomy about my most recent disastrous tryout. "I hit the damn wall several times and impressed the hell out of Cronin. Then he asked me to run the bases. I tried! My knee gave way again. Now I play every Sunday in the Boston Park League. I'm a star. They allow me a pinch runner and I can stay in the game."

Rudy displayed a puzzled stare. "So you must play there pretty damn well for our team to sign you. Do you pitch too?"

I allowed my mind to linger. *The truth might blow my chance at solving the missing ballplayer mystery*, I thought to myself. "Not as well as Steve Majors," I said. "By the way, what the hell happened to him? I understand he was rooming with you and then disappeared last week?"

Perspiration broke out on Rudy's brow. He coughed and quickly drained half of his water glass. "I - I don't know what happened. He's a kook, you know. I might drink too much, but I can still play. This kid was high all the time in Spring Training."

We ordered hamburgers.

Rudy asked for a draft beer.

"How are you at keeping secrets?" I finally asked, investigating the idea of taking Rudy into my confidence since I had already spilled the beans about my bad knee. The aging Indian didn't appear to have any grudges against Majors, and if I could get in cahoots with one of the ballplayers, well ---? And my father, a cop, had taught me that guilty people clam up when questioned. "Do you have a warrant?" "I'm calling my lawyer!" And innocent people can't tell you enough. Rudy already was covered with innocents.

I asked, "Before you answer that question, did you like Majors?"

Rudy blew the foam off his beer glass. It fell onto some fake flowers decorating the table. "H.G. Wells died yesterday and I didn't tell anybody," he said with a chuckle. "So that takes care of the secret question. And Majors never tried to mess with my women. My girlfriends are usually Indian ascendants and they all drink too much. Birds of a feather, you know. So no, he never made me jealous of his smooth talk and sexy walk."

I decided to change the subject - for a moment. "What do you know about Mr. Yawkey's secretary, Penny Michaels?"

Rudy guzzled his draft and filled his mouth with half the burger, hesitated, and then - "She's cute, smart, and a flirt. Mr.

Yawkey doesn't fool around with her and Majors propositioned her every chance he got. Majors bragged to me just last week that he'd nail her if it was the last thing he ever did. Maybe it was! He disappeared, ya know."

I reflected on Rudy's remarks. Somebody put a nickel in the jukebox and played the popular wartime tune - **Don't Sit Under The Apple Tree With Anyone Else But Me.** "Maybe you're right. Mr. Yawkey told me that Majors was your roommate up 'till last week. Then I guess the kid was supposed to pitch tomorrow."

Rudy sat up straight and widened his droopy eyes. "I doubt he'll show up for the game. I'm sure the kid's stoned somewhere, or he met some hot broad and he's screwing her brains out. Actually, not a bad idea."

I hesitated before responding. "Mr. Yawkey doesn't think so. For some reason he thinks there's been foul play. He says that a lot of the ballplayers hated the kid, and Majors hasn't even showed up at the park for a week."

Rudy fumbled in his shirt pocket for a cigarette. I handed him a Chesterfield. "Maybe he's right," Rudy said. "He was the most egotistical prick I ever met. Why'd you ask me if I could keep a secret?"

I decided to answer, this time honestly. "I'm not supposed to tell anyone, but for some reason I trust you to keep a secret. I'm a private detective looking into what happened to Majors. Some of us shamuses need a sidekick. You know, Dr. Watson and Sherlock Holmes? Pat Patton and Dick Tracy? Batman and Robin?"

Rudy raised his palm like a traffic cop. "Yeah, yeah, I know. Okay, I'll be your sidekick. You Lone Ranger, me Indian companion Tonto."

"Okay Tonto, your first assignment is to try and stay sober. It'll help the Sox win games and help me find out what happened. And, by all means, don't tell anyone our secret."

Rudy looked down at the crumbs on his plate. "Maybe I'll have another. This time a hotdog! The Babe ate a lot of 'em and he's in the Hall of Fame."

I leaned back in my chair and stared out of the window onto Kenmore Square. People milled in and out of the trolley stop across the street. In a few hours the area would be mobbed with fans. "Does Penny go to all the games?"

Rudy smiled. "You got a crush on her already? She is a knockout."

I removed the five hundred dollar check from my wallet and placed it in front of my new pal. "Read the back."

The big Indian did, and then looked up with wide saucer eyes. "It's obvious she's got a boner for you. What are you gonna do about it?"

"Call her after the game, I guess. An investigator has to start somewhere. In a murder case, if this turns out to be that, everyone is a suspect. Even you, and even Mr. Yawkey. But I already crossed him out because he admitted that Majors took a shot at his wife Jean, and so I deduce no way would he hire a detective to investigate, even a cheap one like me." I handed my new roommate the team's bio book with all the players along with the rest of the employees.

York flipped a few pages and stopped. "Well, um, I coulda killed the prick. I had to room with him for a week, although it was like rooming with a suitcase. He wasn't around very much. And if I were you, I wouldn't cross Mr. Yawkey's name off the list too fast. He has every right to be pissed off after helping the kid, and then being let down."

"You're too nice a guy, Rudy. I don't think you'd even swat a fly. Would you?"

Rudy showed all his teeth in smile. "Spiders yes, but I shoo innocent flies out the window. You're best bet might be to start ---? He flipped by a few pages. "Yeah, with Roy Partee. He's our back-up catcher. He didn't beat Majors up - just threatened to kill him with a baseball bat when he caught him flirting with his wife, Edith. From what I understand Majors wasn't doing anything bad - just kidding around. Flirting! The kid was a big kidder. He'd tickle the women. Stuff like that. I really don't know why Partee got so upset. Maybe it was his own insecurity. I think his wife did like Majors. Hell, all the skirts liked him. And Partee was in the Army as a munitions guy."

I did a doubled-take at Rudy's insight. *Maybe the big Indian is smarter than he pretends to be.* "Mr. Yawkey said that one of the guys caught Majors in bed with the player's girlfriend. Who was that?"

Rudy waived to the waiter for another draft. "You want to join me?" he asked with almost a pleading look.

"Yeah!" I finally gave in. "Can't let Indian drink firewater alone."

Rudy relaxed his jowls and turned a few pages. "That's Tex. Tex Hughson. Probably our best lefty pitcher in years. Maybe the best lefty in the league. He's gonna win 20 this year. Mark my words."

"What happened?" I asked and took the book back from York, checking Hughson's bio, reading to myself.

The ace southpaw had come to the Sox in 1941 and won 22 leaving the Red Sox in the beginning of September of 1944. That season he had already won 18 games and was called away in the middle of a hot pennant race. It probably cost the team Mr. Yawkey's first championship. Apparently the Draft Board wasn't a fan of baseball, Hughson, or the Red Sox.

Rudy grabbed the bill, studied it, threw some money on the table, and began sipping his draft. "He's also a ladies man. You know the type. Well, he caught Majors in bed with his latest girlfriend. It wasn't like they were married, or anything like that. He had met her during Spring Training and probably would have never seen her again after the season started. I've had a few of those romances."

I began working on my beer. "And Hughson socked him one?"

"More than one! A few of us heard the commotion, interceded, and had to pull him off or he might've killed the kid.

Majors didn't even defend himself. Guess he has a self-confidence issue also. Hey, maybe we all do."

Rudy finished off his drink, licked the foam off his wide lips and remarked cautiously, "I don't want to get anyone in trouble, you know. We got a pennant to clinch. If it turns out that a bunch of the guys ganged up on the kid. Well ---?"

I leaned forward. "Well, what? Is that what happened? Maybe an accident?"

Rudy put one hand over his mouth and whispered. "We was all in a Florida bar this Spring. The kid came in with some floozy. We started teasing. She began to cry and left. I guess we got pretty rowdy. But the kid shouldn't have acted that way."

"What way?"

"Majors walked up to the table without saying a word, and then studied us guy's faces. His eyes were glazed over. I'm sure he was stoned. He zeroed in on Mace Brown, an older pitcher on the squad, but a real nice man. Hell, he hadn't said a word. Majors picked up a table knife and jammed it into the top of Brown's left hand. Good thing he's a righty or his career woulda been over right then and there. If I were Mace I'da killed the kid right there and then."

I quickly perused Brown in the notebook. The right-handed pitcher was born in North English, Iowa 1910 making him on the older side for an athlete. He came to the Sox in 1942 as a reliever. Mace has been married since 1930. He had a quiet personality and was popular with his teammates. My piqued interest brought my head closer to Rudy's whispering lips. "Yeah, then what? Who went after him?"

"A couple of the guys wanted to beat the shit outta him and even said so out loud. I pushed them back into their seats and went to look for the kid. He was outside in the parking lot throwing up and crying. I slapped him on the face a couple of times and told him to go back to the hotel. That's the night he got arrested for drunken driving. Guess I shoulda taken him home. But, at least no one killed him that night."

I took in a deep breath. A clock on the restaurant wall read almost two. "We gotta get ready for a ballgame, Rudy. How are you feeling? Want some coffee?"

Rudy nodded and motioned the waiter back to the table.

I ordered two strong black coffees.

CHAPTER FIVE

BOSTON POST HEADLINES 1946

BOB FELLER SETS ALL-TIME STRIKEOUT RECORD

TED WILLIAMS OFFERED $500,000 TO PLAY IN MEXICAN LEAGUE

MR. YAWKEY POUNDED HIS POINTER FINGER on his intercom button and called to his secretary. "Can you hear me Penny. Hello! Hello!"

He had purchased the new fangled machine on her say-so and had almost mastered the button that said SEND, and the other one that said RECEIVE. More often than not he got them mixed up and yelled into an empty microphone. "Please bring me some ice, dear. It's time for a highball."

Within seconds she bounded into the office with a bucket of ice and some crackers. He was a man of habit, and even if he hadn't called her she would have brought him his daily desire right on the button. She fluttered her eyelashes, a habitual flirt thing, and then filled his glass with ice and poured straight scotch. She then crushed a fresh strawberry to give it taste and handed it to him. "Enjoy," she purred like a kitten.

"You may join me if you like. I'd like to ask you a few questions about Steve Majors. I know he was bothering you, but you are an awful flirt."

She forced a smile and sat in the easy chair. "I hated him," she mumbled. "He even forced his way into my apartment last week. I didn't dare tell you that."

Mr. Yawkey flashed a look of revulsion. "You should have, dear. I have to know those things. I can't fix something if I don't know it's broken."

Penny lowered her head. "I thought you might fire him if I did, and I knew you were counting on his arm to help win the pennant." She began to sob uncontrollably.

The Red Sox owner arose from his chair and walked around the desk giving her his handkerchief. "Now, now, take is easy my dear. You know that I think of you as the daughter I never had."

She forced a smile.

"He won't bother you anymore," he said, paused and frowned. "Maybe he won't bother anyone anymore. Did you do something to him to get him upset?"

"The other way around," she whispered through a new wave of tears.

"What do you mean?"

She removed a lacy hanky from her purse and blew her nose. "Do I have to tell you?"

"Not if you don't want to my dear. But it might help us get to the bottom of things. Besides, confession is good for the soul. I think! A Catholic Priest once told me that. Don't Catholics confess all their sins every Saturday and get forgiven?"

Penny shrugged and closed her eyes, seemed to meditate for a few minutes, opened them wide, and the words began tumbling out. "He came over to my apartment the other night. Actually eight days ago. I was already asleep. He leaned on the buzzer until I answered. He told me it was raining and he was soaked. He sounded okay and I figured he wouldn't dare try anything funny because of you. I thought that he'd be afraid you'd fire him if he did, so I unlocked the latch. It was 10 AM and I grabbed a wooly bathrobe to cover my negligee. I went into the kitchen and flipped on the stove to warm up some coffee. A firm hand on my shoulder startled me."

"Hey, cutie pie," I heard him say in an unsteady voice suggesting he was high. And I could smell alcohol on his breath. I spun around and faced him. Sometimes his harmless but attractive looks hid his dope and alcohol-induced mean streak. He was wearing a white tight T-shirt with the Red Sox logo on the front. Maybe he thought that was a ticket to my – well, you know. You're a man! Then I pushed him away and quickly accused him of being on something. I told him to sit down and I'd give him some coffee. He sat but started to playfully tug on my bathrobe sash, allowing the front to fall open. He wolf-whistled at the sight." She hesitated and covered her face with her opened palm hands. "I can't continue with this Mr. Yawkey. I'm too embarrassed. Nothing really happened, although he did rough me up trying."

The owner shrugged and then nodded. "Eight days ago, heh? Did he then leave?"

Penny hesitated and then shook her head. "I wish he did, but then he had the gall to invite me to smoke some reefer with him, and he admitted that he was already wasted. Several times I suggested that he leave. I told him I was tired and wanted to go back to bed. He tried to blame me for everything. The creep! He accused me of flirting with him during Spring Training. I took Psyche 101 in college and learned that when people turn things around like that its call Projection. Real scary to know someone like that who takes no responsibility for his or her own actions. Our teacher told us if you ever get involved with someone like that - run, run, run!"

"You are a flirt," Mr. Yawkey said.

Penny wiped her eyes with a fluffy pink hanky. "Please don't defend him. If he hadn't left that night I think I would've found a knife and killed him. I knew what he wanted, and no way was I giving it to him. You know what he had the audacity to say before he left?"

The boss shook his head, but leaned forward as not to miss a word of the juicy true confession.

"He said that all you males know that NO means YES, and that the population in the country would only be half if horny guys took NO for an answer. I insisted that my NO meant NO and that I was engaged to someone else. And then I promised not to tell you about what had happened if he would leave immediately."

"I blame myself for being so lenient on him after Spring Training. I should have had him committed to some rehab hospital and paid the bill until he was cured. Instead, I hired a private doctor. I was being totally selfish - only thinking about the bad publicity. You've told me enough and I totally understand. But it seems like you might have been the last person to see him. As far as I know, no one has heard from him since that night."

Penny rounded her shoulders and clasped her hands tightly together. Her eyes were watering. "I'm glad he's gone and I am so sorry for you and your patient with him. He's a creep! I think he's nuts. He's not even human. I think I would've killed him if he had done what he wanted."

"Why don't you go home early today, my dear? I'll close up the office. We're playing the Browns at four. Should be an easy win. I'll see you in the morning. And don't worry. I don't think you'll have to worry about Mr. Majors any longer."

CHAPTER SIX

BOSTON POST HEADLINES 1946

SYRIA'S INDEPENDENCE GAINED FROM FRANCE

28 JAP LEADERS INDICTED FOR WAR CRIMES

RUDY AND I ARRIVED ON THE FIELD AT THREE O'CLOCK. I nervously was introduced to the players during batting practice. Ted Williams, the league's batting leader was most polite by giving me a few batting tips after I swung and missed several times in the practice cage. My well-bandaged knee wobbled as my loyal Uncle Bill called encouragement from a front row box. He was seated quite comfortably in his wheel chair sucking on an orange filled with liquor – a trick he had learned from the recently deceased famous movie comic W.C. Fields. I checked my notebook on Ted who was born 1918 in San Diego, California - some now calling him the greatest hitter of all time. Ted batted .406 in 1941, and then missed the 1942, 1943, 1944 and 1945 seasons as a fighter pilot in the U.S. Marines.

"You're dropping your right elbow," Ted advised. "You'll never get a hit in this league doing that."

I corrected my swing and hit the left field wall on the next three pitches. Rudy patted me on the back when I returned to the dugout. "You got a nice swing, kid. Maybe you are a ballplayer."

Rudy chewed some gum to keep the alcohol smell away from his breath. The game started at four and the Brown's pitcher Jack Kramer lasted five innings before being lifted for a pinch hitter. The Sox teed off on a string of three relievers in the last three innings, eventually scoring fifteen runs to the Brown's six. Williams, York, and Doerr homered. I didn't play, but got to friend-up with some of the players in the dugout, especially Leon Culberson, a utility outfielder. "So I hear that the team signed some great fastball kid this spring who was supposed to pitch tomorrow. Where the heck is he?"

Culberson frowned. "That fuckin' prick? Stevie boy Majors! He exposed himself to my girlfriend at Spring Training. Asshole! He shoulda been arrested."

"You're kidding," I pretended to be surprised. "Why would he do that? Drunk?"

"More than drunk. Stoned! I told 'im if he ever even looked at her again, I'd kill 'im."

"Shit," I thought. *"Another suspect. How the hell do the real private eyes solve these things? On the other hand, Culberson didn't ask me for a warrant or ask to see his lawyer. Thanks for the tip, Dad.* I crossed the outfielder off my list.

After the game, back at the Kenmore Hotel, Rudy, Roy Partee, third baseman Mike Higgins, the Browns best slugger Vern Stephens and I sat in the bar sharing stories, drinks, eating supper, and philosophizing on life in general. Stephens didn't imbibe, but admitted to the same demon as Majors. He couldn't keep his eyes or hands off pretty women.

"Looks like you guys have sewed up the pennant," remarked Stephens over a cup of coffee. "What are you now? Fifteen games ahead?"

"I've seen good teams get cocky and blow big leads," Rudy said and chuggle-lugged his draft beer.

"Hey, is it true that that new kid Majors isn't starting tomorrow," Stephens asked. "I was looking forward to seeing him pitch. Striking out 27 batters in one game is quite a accomplishment in any league."

"He disappeared," Higgins said. "Just up and disappeared. Everybody hated the prick anyway. He had issues!"

"Issues? What kind?" asked Stephens. "We all got issues. Hey, I got issues. I love women. All women. I can't help it if I was born with an itchy prick."

Partee cringed, downed his beer, and left the table, taking a stool at the bar.

I followed! I had investigating to do. He had been nice to me in the dugout. "Mind if I join you?"

"Not a bit," Partee said, apparently cooled off.

I waved to the bartender who served another patron and then approached us. "Drinks?"

"Draft," I said. "Roy?"

The catcher nodded. "Make it two and put it on my tab." He smiled at me. "I got a running tab with the bar. This is where I live when we're home. I have a house down South and my wife stays there with my son."

"I heard about Majors," I said. "Sorry! I guess he's a real pain in the ass."

The bartender brought two drafts.

I sipped.

Partee guzzled.

"It was no big deal," Partee said. "The kid thinks he's God's gift to women."

"And?"

"And he got a little too friendly with my wife at Spring Training. Actually, we'd had a spat that night. With my wife, I mean. She's young and pretty. Won some beauty contests before I married her."

"Sounds like you're not putting the complete blame on Majors."

Partee guzzled some more and shrugged. "My old man gave me some marriage advice once. Maybe I shoulda taken it."

"And what was that?"

"Marry an ugly woman. So if she ever leaves you, you won't miss her."

I grinned and analyzed the advice. "Did your Dad follow his own advice?"

Partee paused – and then answered. "I'm not sure. He had been married three times by the time he settled down with my mother."

"Was she pretty?"

"I thought so. But now that I think of it, she had buck teeth."

"Better than no teeth at all," I mumbled as I digested Partee's information. "It's none of my business, but did other guys come onto your wife?"

Partee nodded to the query and again to the bartender. "I'm not catching tomorrow so I can have a few extras."

"So you'd have no reason to knock Majors off," I popped a surprise question that even surprised me. I had never investigated a suspected murder before, but reminded myself of movies and radio shows that always waited 'till the final scene to reveal the killer. I didn't want to wait that long.

Partee straightened up and frowned. "Are you kidding? The punk's not worth killing. Why? Did someone say he was dead? None of us have seen him all week."

"I – um –, I don't know. He was supposed to pitch tomorrow I thought, and I guess he's gone missing."

Partee shook his head. "The kid's a pothead. That's why he was left in Florida. Great ability! His fastball hurt my hand. If he's missing, I'm sure he's back on the reefers - or more stuff."

I finished my draft. "Thanks for the drink, Roy. I'm going back to the table. See you tomorrow. Maybe I'll get to pinch hit."

I returned to the table and sat down beside Rudy, took out my notebook and crossed off Partee's name. He couldn't tell me enough!

"Is Roy okay?" Rudy asked, slurring his words. "I think he's a bit thin-skinned. Let's shoot some darts for drinks."

The Kenmore bar featured an old cork dartboard in a dingy corner.

"I don't think I should," I said.

"Why not? Scared of us veterans?" Third baseman Higgins asked with a sneer. I had checked on his profile, and he appeared to be an asshole.

"Not really," I answered and glanced at York. "I'm like a pro. It wouldn't be fair to you guys. I'm just trying to be honest."

Higgins let out a stupid laugh. "Pro? My ass! There ain't no pros in darts. I'm pretty good myself, if I do say so myself. I'll double any bets against you, Rook."

I stood up. "What are the stakes, Mr. Higgins? I have about a half hour before my bedtime. Remember, I am a rookie, so let's make it quick." Sometimes I could act like an asshole, and I was never proud of it.

Higgins wiped some perspiration off his brow and guzzled the dregs of his beer glass. "Draft beers are a dime. How about you and I have a private bet of ten bucks? And the loser also buys everyone a drink."

I smirked and nodded.

The group all moved to a far corner booth.

Higgins shot first. Four darts! The bulls-eye was ten points. It was tiny - maybe an inch in diameter. The board was fifteen feet away. He waggled his hand, and then threw.

Bulls-eye!

He cracked a sly smirk.

His second shot missed, but not by much. It was an eight.

His third fell off the board.

"Faulty dart," he said. "Doesn't count!"

"Yes it does," York interceded. "We all shoot the same darts."

"Fuck you, Redskin," Higgins mumbled under his breath and fired the last dart into the wall. "I got eighteen. First round! Let's see you guys beat that. The last time I threw darts was during Spring Training against that asshole Majors. His arrogance was like yours – Dark."

"Who won that match?" I asked.

"The punk was drunk or stoned. I didn't know which, and didn't really care."

"So?" I asked.

"I beat the shit outta him in the darts game, and then he stiffed me. At least twenty bucks! I swore to myself that I'd get even. But he never showed up 'till a few weeks ago, and then one night I met him at the Kenmore Hotel bar and asked him for the money. The prick told me to go fuck myself."

"And?" I asked thinking that a drunk Higgins would confess to murder and the case would be over. *Fat chance!*

"It was last week sometime. He acted stoned. I grabbed his throat and told him to pay or I'd break his wrist. Pitchers don't like broken wrists."

Higgins gulped down several gulps, grinned and patted my shoulder. "Don't worry Dark. I'm sure that prick ain't as good a dart thrower as you. You hope!"

York then set himself up in front of the board, wound up like a pitcher and threw. He missed the bulls-eye four times, but scored on all his shots. He went forward to collect the darts and removed them, counting. "Sixteen," he announced.

Stephens then stepped up, winked at me and flipped in one bulls-eye, and then missed with the other three darts. "Too much caffeine," he said. "I got a shitty ten."

He retrieved the darts and handed them to me. I began by squinting my eyes and studying the board. The corner of the room was dusky - sort of like Halloween. I stared at the points and feathers, weighed the first dart in my hand, and then threw – an easy flip of the wrist.

Bull's-eye!

I half smiled, hesitated, thought about Yawkey's fountain pen, and then fired in my second bull's-eye.

"That's twenty already," York excitedly said. "Show 'em what you're made of, kid. I hope Pinky can afford to lose."

Higgins frowned and gulped on his beer.

I quickly threw two more bulls-eyes - the first one splitting one of the darts.

"Shit man, where did you learn to shoot like that?" Stephens asked. "You could turn pro if they had a dart's league. Maybe the Olympics?"

I smiled! "I tried to tell you guys that I could shoot darts. Worked at a carnival one summer with the knife thrower. Hey, everybody is good at something – I think. And I'm good at darts."

I put my open palm in front of Higgins. "Ten bucks, please. And if you're a real gentleman you'll pick up the tab for everyone - the price you have to pay for doubting my ability."

Higgins scowled and jammed a ten spot into my hand, gave everyone else the finger and skulked out of the bar.

"Thanks," Rudy whispered to me. "You flushed his john."

I seriously believed the fun evening wasn't a waste. I had already crossed out Partee's name, and now I eliminated Higgins. No way would he tell the story about threatening Majors if he had harmed the kid in any way.

Stephens waved to the waitress - a young, cute, cheap appearing girl. Too much makeup and too much perfume! He flashed a handsome smile. She returned it and made her way to the booth. St. Louis was in town for one more day, and Stephens obviously needed some female companionship.

"I'll have another coffee," the St. Louis shortstop said and locked in on her brown eyes.

"Better check her ID," Rudy whispered. "She looks underage, and you don't want to spend tomorrow's game in jail."

Stephens laughed. "I never do anything stupid. People with my addiction never take any chances. I don't need a case of the Crabs."

I suddenly remembered the note I'd received from Mr. Yawkey's secretary. The clock over the bar read eight. Curfew was midnight. I excused myself, winked at Rudy and headed for a pay phone. I found Penny Michaels' number, inserted a nickel into the slot and dialed.

After several rings a woman's peppy voice answered. "If you're selling something, I gave at the office."

"Sorry Penny. This is Penny, isn't it?"

"Yeah! And who's this?"

"Johnny Dark. You gave me your number on the back of Mr. Yawkey's check. I thought maybe you had something important to tell me. I would've called earlier but I've been hanging with some of the boys in the hotel."

Penny giggled. "Like you're a real player?"

I hesitated. "That's not the point. Did Mr. Yawkey tell you why I'm on the team? No one is supposed to know."

"He didn't, but I got A in eavesdropping. I know everything about the team and Mr. Yawkey. Do you want to come over and give me the third degree?"

"I – um, I guess so. I'm at the Kenmore. Where do you live?"

"Not far! An apartment on Commonwealth Avenue! 2001. About six blocks from where you're staying. Ring the buzzer and I'll let you in."

She hung up before I could agree or not.

I went back to the bar. Rudy and Stephens were debating whether men could achieve multiple orgasms like women. I threw a couple of dollars on the table. "This should cover my drinks. Hey, I'd like to hang around and find out the answers. I figure Stephens here has probably found out - or is on a quest to find out – maybe even write a book."

Rudy smiled and patted me on the butt. "Don't be late. Curfew's at midnight. Do you know about the birds and the bees? Mr. Yawkey asked me to look out for you."

"I thought it was the other way around," I said with a wide grin. "The bee stings the bird under her feathers. Or is it the other way around?"

CHAPTER SEVEN

BOSTON POST HEADLINES 1946

RED SOX PESKY SCORES 6 RUNS IN ONE GAME

1ST US ROCKET LEAVES ATMOSPHERE 50 MILES UP

I JOGGED UP COMMONWEALTH AVENUE counting the old buildings until I reached 2001, several minutes later. It was a typical August New England night. Lots of bright stars in a clear sky, small clean smelling breeze, light late-evening city traffic, and a few dog walkers bidding every other walker a "good evening". *Life is good,* I thought to myself. *But maybe not for Majors.*

Penny's abode was a large, three-story brownstone. Probably a very expensive home in the late 1800s and recently turned into numerous apartments. *Maybe I'm in the wrong racket,* I pondered. *I should be a property owner.* A guy named Leavitt was building cheep slab homes in Pennsylvania and selling them like hotcakes to the GIs. They're even naming the town after him – Levittown. I could do that. *Darktown! No – Johnnytown. Dream on, asshole!*

I walked up the stone front steps, checked the directory and pressed the APT. 1 buzzer, and then said my name into the speaker. It immediately buzzed back and I heard the lock click.

I opened the door and looked down a long, high ceiling dim hallway – and then started walking. The first door on the right was APT. 1. It appeared thick, wooden, and unbreakable. Safe! I knocked! It was already open a crack, so I pushed it all the way into what appeared to be a spacious, probably the original living room. High ceilings, it featured an enormous fireplace with no fire, built-in bookshelves with no books, and several heavily curtained windows overlooking the outside dimly lighted street. Penny, dressed in a silky white bathrobe, sat on a long sofa seemingly listening to a console radio. The news! "And so today marks the opening in theaters all over the country of Humphrey Bogart and Lauren Bacall's new film, The Big Sleep. On the boxing front, the man who almost dethroned heavyweight champion, Joe Lewis, Billy Conn has retired."

I forced a cough. "I'm here, Miss Mitchell. May I come in?"

She jumped, turned around and smiled. "Of course." She flipped off the radio, got up and walked to greet me with a handshake. "Coffee or something else? I'm having black coffee. Anyone ever tell you that you look like a tall version of Alan Ladd? You should dye your hair blonde and the girls would swoon over you."

She was barefooted, wearing silk tennis shorts, a white collared tennis top, three buttons opened at the neck. I felt my heart almost stop beating. *Am I having a heart attack?* I asked myself. *Tough guys don't have heart attacks at my age.*

"Black coffee will be fine," I heard myself say. I suddenly felt like a schoolboy with my first crush. I couldn't take my eyes away from Penny's eyes. *Am I blinking? Is she blinking? I wonder what she tastes like.*

She moistened her lips with the tip of her tongue and smiled, got up and left the room to fetch the coffee.

Directly over the reddish brick fireplace I noticed a life-size oil portrait of Penny hanging on a sky blue wall- papered wall. The young face looked down at me through hooded eyelids. My heart pounded even faster. The entire scene reminded me of the movie Laura. I felt a small consolation knowing that

Penny was very much alive. The Laura movie PI had to wait almost an hour to find that Gene Tierney was alive, and then fell further in love.

Penny returned a few minutes later carrying a wooden tray offering coffee and plain donuts. "I thought you might be hungry," she said. "I am!"

She sat down a few feet from me on the multi-colored pillowed couch, studied my staring, and then asked, "Are you okay?"

I wasn't okay, but nodded my head anyway. "I was hoping you could tell me about Steve Majors," I finally said, took a bite out of a donut, and ceased ogling.

"Probably could tell you a lot," she said and daintily took one of the donuts and nibbled.

"Is that a painting of you over the mantel?" I asked.

"Yup! My graduation gift from my parents. They love art and knew a famous local artist. I posed for too many days. He even asked me to lower my blouse. I refused, of course. And I didn't tell my parents. Do you think all photographers and painters ask girls to disrobe?"

I hadn't been privy to the acquaintance of many painters or photographers, or even many dirty old men, so I withheld my opinion. *But not a bad idea,* I thought and perused the portrait again trying to imagine what Penny would look like without the top. The artist had depicted her with a frilly, off-the-shoulder black blouse, low enough to hint at ample bosoms. I liked it and began to feel aroused. "I really think he did a swell job," I finally commented. "I didn't take any art courses in high school. And I won't take up a lot of your time."

Penny reached for another donut, curled her feet up under her bottom and moved a cushion closer to me.

"How old are you?" she asked in a soft voice.

"Twenty-six. Why?"

"I don't know. When I think of private eyes I think of Humphrey Bogart in the Maltese Falcon. He looks older than you. Tougher! Rougher! Are you married?" She was flirting.

I felt like I was going to choke on my coffee, so I decided to quickly change the subject. "I'm single! Now about Majors."

She smiled. "Ever get close - like engaged, or something?"

I cleared my throat, feeling very uncomfortable in the presence of this magnificent specimen of womanhood. Being a man who deliberately avoided relationships I was used to one-night stands. Mixing business with pleasure? Not wise! "Maybe, once," I admitted. "But I was a cop then. Cops who get married end up in divorce court. How would you like to kiss your husband goodbye in the morning and not know if he was ever coming back alive?"

"Sounds like an excuse to not commit?"

"Commitments? How close have you gotten to a commitment?"

She perked up her nose and lifted her eyebrows and sing-songed, "I'm engaged!"

That remark did something bad to my newly fragile inner feelings. *I feel like cupid has shot an arrow through my heart. I've never flipped over a gal this fast in my life. Infatuation?* "Sounds serious!" I said in a strange undertone. *I haven't even been to the plate with this girl, and I already feel as if I've struck out.*

She yawned and rubbed her eyes. "Let's talk about Majors. He chased me around the desk more than once."

"Does your fiancée know about Majors?" I asked, removed my personal notebook and started taking notes, appearing very officious.

Without any warning the front window smashed as some small object flew through it into the center of the room. We both jumped up and looked in the direction of the crash. I instinctively leapt against Penny, knocking her back onto the divan, and then crawled behind it, searching for whatever was thrown through the window. A big bird?

I found it and it wasn't a bird. "A d - damn hand grenade," I muttered in panic mode. "Pull the throw pillows on top of you - quick," I sternly ordered, and then bounded up, grabbed the small grenade, about the size of a baseball, but shaped like a football, and ran into Penny's bathroom. I jammed it into the toilet, grabbed all the towels I could find and crammed them inside on top of the explosive device. I then closed the lid and ran back into the living room, jumped on top of Penny, and dragged her down behind the divan.

"After the pin is pulled the grenade is supposed to go off in several seconds," he said. "Maybe that one's a dud."

We both shivered together and waited.

"What, what happened?" she gasped.

"Nothing yet. Just stay down. I don't know how powerful they are."

Penny began to sob.

"Where's the phone?" I asked.

Her trembling finger pointed to the top of a console radio.

I crawled across the floor, reached up and pulled the phone over to the coffee table, put it to my ear and dialed zero. "Get me the police. It's an emergency."

CHAPTER-EIGHT

BOSTON POST HEADLINES 1946

ASSAULT WINS BELMONT STAKES AND TRIPLE CROWN

1ST BIKINI BATHING SUIT ON DISPLAY IN PARIS

A HALF HOUR LATER THE POLICE HAD ARRIVED IN FORCE, along with a bomb squad. They had carefully taken the grenade away explaining that the water in the toilet had obviously soaked into the ignite action and deadened it.

"Lucky kids," the lead officer said. His name was Murphy - an old pal of mine - my idol when I was on the force. Murph had stayed and I had quit. I was never good at obeying orders – especially stupid ones. We also both played on the same baseball team in the Park League.

Murph had blazing red hair and a temper to go with it. He usually kept the temper in check until an umpire called a strike against him that he deemed a ball. He was polite in his questioning realizing that Penny was frightened out of her wits. "I'll leave you guys alone for now," he said and winked at me.

"Drop by the precinct in the morning. Ten o'clock. I'll leave a man outside the apartment building for the night."

Alone once again, Penny poured two glasses of gin on ice. "Guess someone has it in for you, Johnny," she said and sipped.

"Me? I doubt it! Someone has it in for you. I hate to tell you this, but no one knew where I was going tonight - except Rudy, my roommate. Nope dear, that grenade was meant to silence you - not me. Sorry!"

I could feel the cushion begin to shake from Penny's nerves. "Steve Majors?" she groaned. "I can't believe he'd try to have me killed."

"Why do you think it could be Majors?" I questioned. "Mr. Yawkey thinks Majors might be dead."

"I know! I know! I made Mr. Yawkey purchase that intercom. It was so I could eavesdrop on him. I figured out how to rig it so I can press a button and hear everything going on in his office. A good secretary has to know what's going on, you know. That's how I knew how to spell your name on the check and that you weren't a real ballplayer." She gulped her drink. "Majors is a monster," she stammered. "He chased me around the desk right from the first introduction. Drove me nuts at Spring Training. He was easy to know. No mystery man. A sick puppy, but a good fast ball."

"And that's what Mr. Yawkey cared mostly about?"

"Apparently! He's trying to win a pennant, you know. I told him I could take care of myself."

"And can you?" I asked and glanced across the room at the broken window.

Penny buried her head in her hands, her body balled up in a fetal position. The tears began to flow. I moved beside her and began hugging. "I'm sorry Penny. I'm not trying to upset you with these questions."

She pulled closer to me. "I've got an older brother who protects me," she muttered.

"Against what? He wasn't around tonight when you needed him."

She unwound herself, sat up and adjusted her shorts and shirt. "And my fiancée protects me." She sounded very defensive.

I leaned back and gave her a serious glare. "Look Penny, I want you to comprehend this - now. If that grenade hadn't been drowned in the toilet it would've blown the crap out of this apartment and killed both of us. Someone isn't just playing silly games. And all your so-called bodyguards were nowhere near enough to help. My guess is that this is all tied together with Majors' disappearance. Want to tell me about him? Maybe we can prevent something like this from happening again."

She lay back and placed her head in my lap, face up, pursing her lips.

I glanced at the painting over the fireplace. *Gene Tierney*, I thought. *Probably Hollywood's most beautiful star. Damn!* I felt my heart skip.

Penny interrupted my docile thoughts with a shocking revelation. "He tried to rape me," she confessed, matter of factly. "Eight nights ago. I haven't seen him since."

I quickly digested the revealing information. *Rape? Poor kid!* Through my eyes she suddenly looked like some fragile breakable doll. I felt detestation for Majors - a man I'd never met, but was slowly getting to know and hate. "Did your fiancée know? Who else did you tell?"

She paused, and then said, "Yes! I probably shouldn't have told anyone. But I did. Nash, Mr. Yawkey, and my brother."

I began gently rubbing my fingers through her hair. "Tell me about your fiancée. You say his name is Nash? Do you love him?"

She hesitated again, this time a bit longer, but she didn't tell me to stop the hair massage. "I met him through my brother. They both frequent the horse track. He's nice to me. Gives me lots of gifts. Takes me to nice places for dinner. We've been dating ever since last winter."

I mentally noted that she avoided answering the love question. I reached over her and grabbed the phone off the coffee table. "Here, call your brother."

"Why him? I'm sure he's asleep."

"Please! Just do it! If he's home, ask him if he knows where Majors is."

Penny shrugged and dialed. She patiently waited, and then looked at me for further instructions. "It's almost midnight and he's only 25 years old. He's probably out having a drink with the boys."

"Okay! Hang up and call your fiancée."

She made a face. "Are you nuts? I'm sure he's asleep. Besides, he's out of town."

"Where out of town? And doing what?"

"Now you sound like a detective. He's in New York, and he's a bond salesman."

"Where in New York?

Penny sounded angry, her words clipped. "The Waldorf, if it's anyone's business."

"Call!"

She shrugged again and dialed New York Information, asked for the number of the Waldorf Hotel, and then dialed it. "Donald Nash, please."

She paused, frowned, and spoke harshly. "That's Donald with a D - like the duck. He's from Boston with B like a buck. I know he's registered there. Look again!"

She began tapping her painted fingernails on the coffee table, and then slammed down the phone and gave me a quizzical look. "Maybe I misunderstood him. I thought he said The Waldorf."

I slowly removed the phone from Penny's trembling hands. "It's okay! I'm making you do all the detective work. It's late! We've been through a lot. Why don't you try and get some sleep. The police left a man outside for protection. You have nothing to worry about."

Penny yawned. "Johnny," she purred, would you do me a big favor?"

"Anything," I said, fluffing up one of the softer pillows and placing it under her head.

"Stay! The divan is comfortable and I'll be right in the next room. I'd feel a lot safer if you stayed. And I'm sure Mr. Yawkey would approve."

I knew it was late and that there was nothing I could do to solve the case before morning. "Thanks for inviting me, Penny. If you want me I'll be right here. Tomorrow is another day."

She turned her head away and mumbled, "I saw that movie. Maybe we can go to the flicks sometime. I'd like to see Lauren Bacall and Humphrey." She yawned again. "Did you know she's only like my age? How old did you say you were?"

She was flirting again.

I started to answer when I heard her deep breathing. I lay back, my feet touching her feet, closed my eyes and began counting sheep jumping over the fences.

CHAPTER NINE

BOSTON POST HEADLINES 1946

RED SOX RUDY YORK HITS 2 GRAND SLAMS IN ONE GAME

MARTIN & LEWIS DISCOVERED AT CLUB 500 IN ATLANTIC CITY

I AWOKE IN A STRANGE ROOM and smelled a wonderful sizzling bacon aroma. That often happened in my houseboat home on the Boston waterfront. I'd lived there with my elderly wheelchair bound Uncle Bill since my father had passed away fifteen years previous. I shook the cobwebs out of my head, glanced at the broken front window, and quickly put two and two together. I had almost died in the arms of a beautiful damsel in distress the night before. I sat up, fumbled for cigarettes, lit one and headed for the bathroom. I entered, removed my shirt, cleaned my upper torso with soap and a washcloth, shaved as best I could with a very tiny woman's razor that left a bunch of cuts on my chin and cheeks. I covered them with pieces of toilet paper. I then brushed my teeth with my finger, combed my hair with Penny's brush, and felt presentable for a new day's adventure. A Major League baseball game topped the list, and the seeking of a missing person ran a close second.

I leaned into the kitchen area and said brightly," Good morning Penny. It is morning - isn't it?"

She looked over from standing in front of the stove where she was scrambling some eggs. She broke out in laughter. "What happened to your face? Looks like you put the wrong end of your body in the toilet."

"Funny, funny. It's eight o'clock. The cops want us to meet them at the precinct by ten."

She nodded!

I took a seat on a stool at a center-island bar. She poured me a cup of hot black coffee. I immediately decided I liked being waited on by an attractive lady, one who seemed to be wearing nothing but a bra and panties under her frilly apron. I studied her stature. The pursed lips, perfect figure, and shoulder-length brunette, dappled hair created the most electrifying female I had ever encountered – accept, of course Gene Tierney. And I had only met her in my dreams and on the silver screen in Laura.

I phone the Kenmore Hotel and left Rudy a message, not wanting to wake him from beauty sleep. Penny and I then small-talked, telling each other about our backgrounds, education, family, hopes and goals - and finally I asked, "What do you see when you look into the mirror?"

She double-taked! "What do you mean? I see me, of course."

"No, I mean, how do you look? Beautiful? Smart? Sensuous? If I were you, no one would be able to tear me away from the mirror."

She giggled and fluttered her eyelashes. "Interesting compliment. Does it ever work on pickups?"

"Never used it before. Is it working on you?"

She appeared to blush, ignoring the embarrassing question.

"Do you know that you flirt?" I asked.

She began serving the eggs and bacon. "I've always been like that. Really and honestly - I'm just trying to be friendly to everyone, and apparently it comes across like flirting. It got me my job with Mr. Yawkey."

I reached out and tenderly touched the top of her hand. "And it may have almost got you killed. You don't have any idea the kind of people who live and die in the city. Hell, you spent a bunch of years in a civilized suburban high school, and then two years at exclusive Katie Gibbs secretarial school. Now you enjoy a Lilly-livered, white career - safely behind the walls of Mr. Yawkey's office. You've lived such a sheltered life. When I spent two years on the Boston police force I met all the scumbags - real nut cases with no morals. And most of them can't even help it. They had no fathers. They began stealing as youngsters just to eat or feed a dope habit. They can't be reasoned with, and that's why the jails are filled with them - and the cemeteries."

She pulled her hand away. "You make it sound so awful. Isn't your work exciting?"

"Yeah! It's real thrilling to stuff a grenade in a toilet."

She ignored the analogy and said, "What do people wear to a police station? I've never been in one."

"Nothing revealing," I answered, lifting my eyebrows and checking out her partially hidden figure under the apron. "Maybe like you'd wear to church."

Penny cleaned her plate with a piece of toast. "Love my cooking?" she briskly asked. "I can make eggs, toast, Kellogg's Pep cold cereal, and warm up leftovers. Do you cook?"

"My uncle does the cooking. I told you about him. Or maybe I didn't. He's my favorite guy - a World War One vet in a wheelchair. He lost a leg over there. He never really tells anyone how it happened. But it earned him a lifetime monthly check from the government. Just about enough to drink too much and take a weekly trip to the racetrack. He brought me up after my father died. And my mother - she – well, that's another matter. Uncle Bill spends a lot of time at the Old Howard burlesque house in Scollay Square, and brings home the corniest jokes. Most of them too dirty to repeat."

"I like him already," she said. "And I'm not too prudish to hear dirty jokes. I am twenty-one."

Penny began cleaning off the table, putting the dishes in the sink. She looked over at me and asked. "Another coffee?"

I shook my head. "We have a date with my pal Murph. Why don't you get dressed and we'll pay him a visit. I don't think you should tell him about the rape attempt."

Penny frowned and looked puzzled. "Why not? That's something he'd want to know."

"And not that I don't trust him to keep it a secret, but it's something that could get into the newspapers. I don't think you or Mr. Yawkey would like that publicity."

"Just wait a sec and I'll get dressed."

I watched intently as she exited the room, her backside uncovered by the apron. *Now I know why Uncle Bill spends so much time at the Old Howard,*" I said to myself. *What a great ass she has.*

CHAPTER TEN

BOSTON POST HEADLINES 1946

PERCEY SPENCER INVENTS MICROWAVE OVEN

BASEBALL GRANTS $5,000 MINIMUM ANNUAL SALARY

PENNY AND I SPENT OVER AN HOUR AT THE PRECINCT, mostly Penny answering questions about who she knew that might want to kill her. She had only lived in the apartment eight months, and one of those months was spent in Florida attending Spring Training camp. She broke into tears several times, but obviously appreciated the steady reassurance of my company, and the fact that I felt at home in the police station. I knew many of the detectives, especially Murphy who went out of his way to be affable. He almost seemed more interested in my playing with the Red Sox than Penny's brush with death. "And you room with Rudy York?" Murph asked and beamed. "Can you get me his autograph?"

I laughed. "I'll get them all for you - on an official baseball. But don't use the damn thing. If the Sox win the World Series the ball will be worth lots of dough someday. Hey, they haven't won since 1918."

When we were dismissed we cabbed to Fenway Park, grabbed two steamed hot-dogs, and went into Mr. Yawkey's office, relaying the evening's and morning's events.

"Do you think Majors might be still alive and tried to kill Penny?" he asked me, breathless with true fear. "Good thing you were around, my boy."

"I don't know what to think, sir, I mean Tom. Penny told me about Major's attempted rape, but I can't figure why he'd try and kill her. Hell, he's smitten by her."

Mr. Yawkey scratched thinning hair. "I agree! Maybe the bomb was meant for you. You must have pissed off a few bad guys in your line of work." He looked at Penny. "Excuse my harsh language, dear."

She smiled. "Harsh things are happening."

"Too harsh," I said. "I have a feeling that whoever threw that grenade has been around Penny's apartment before."

"Why's that?" Penny raised her eyebrows with interest.

"The front door of apartment buildings are always locked - or supposed to be. Your apartment is number ONE, but for someone who doesn't know, it could be on the left, or on the right. Right?"

Mr. Yawkey and Penny thought about the scenario, and then both nodded.

"So," I continued, "the perpetrator must have known Penny's apartment was on the right of the front door."

"Or maybe he was trying to kill my neighbor?" Penny beamed with the thought that would mean no one was after her after all.

I shook my head. "I checked on that, hoping it might be true. But, sorry, the tenant moved out last week. The apartment is empty."

Mr. Yawkey asked Penny to leave the room. "I have some private things to talk about with Mr. Dark and Penny has some letters to write."

Penny nodded, waved bye bye to me, fluttered her eyelashes and left. I knew she'd be listening.

"I have to call the precinct and make sure this story stays out of the newspapers," Mr. Yawkey said. "They like me there, and they know I don't need any bad publicity. Who did you say the lead officer is?"

I gave him Murphy's name and assured him that the newspaper thing had already been taken care of.

The team owner made the call anyway and mentioned something about free box-seat tickets, hung up and smiled. "Thanks! I talked to Murphy and he said you'd taken care of it. But I'm sure he'll enjoy the tickets. Now I've got a favor to ask of you." He leaned over his desk towards me. "I want to pay you a bonus to be Penny's bodyguard. What do you say?"

I never turned down extra cash and always needed it. "I'm sort of her bodyguard already."

"No! I mean stick with her like glue. Either you move in with her, or her with you."

I shivered, shrugged, and flashed a wide grin. "There's nothing I'd like better than to guard her body, sir. But she's engaged. I don't think that would go over very well with her fiancée. Do you?"

Mr. Yawkey chuckled. "Nash? I know that fool. He tries to buy her favors. Throws his money around like confetti. He's at least twenty years her senior. I think he'll end up being a loser. She'll wake up and dump him. I hope! Maybe you can help there, too."

"She thinks he sells bonds."

"Don't tell her I said this," the team owner suggested, sort of in a whisper, "but I doubt he sells anything. More like whatever he does is against the law."

"Why don't you tell her about your suspicions?"

"I tried once. She got very protective. She seems to be surrounded by bums. Her brother doesn't even have a job. He hangs around the race tracks with his hoodlum pals."

A quick knock on the door startled us two men as the door burst opened and Penny bounced into the room. "Hope you two weren't talking about little ole me."

I tipped my head and flashed an observant stare. "Mr. Yawkey wants me to stay with you until this thing blows over."

Penny stood straight, threw her arms back and yawned. It made for a Petty Girl Calendar pose that brought my eyes into full focus. My heart began to pitter-patter again. *Damn her,* I thought. *I don't feel ready for any kind of relationship with a nice person - especially a person already engaged.*

"How will your fiancée handle me staying at your apartment?" I asked, lightly shaking my head so only she could get the message.

She smiled. "After that grenade I don't think I'll be comfortable staying there myself. And he did lie to me about the Waldorf. I have a right to be mad at him. Don't I?"

"And use me to make him jealous? I don't think I like being a pawn for anyone."

Mr. Yawkey butted in. "You're not going to be a pawn, my boy. A king or a knight in shining armor, but not a pawn. Don't forget, you're doing this for me - and I'm paying you handsomely."

I threw my hands in the air in a surrender gesture. "Okay, okay! I give up! You can move in with Uncle Bill and me. He'll love the company. I'm never home anyway."

I glanced at the old grandfather clock. "Noon! I better get on downstairs to the field or they'll be sending me to the minors."

Penny purred! "I'll see you right after the game and we can cab back to my apartment to gather my things."

I looked back at her.

She smiled and winked.

Mr. Yawkey winked.

So I also winked.

Do four winks make a wight? I asked myself. *Funny!*

The ringing of the phone interrupted the happy-go-lucky gathering. Penny picked up. "Who? Yes Detective Murphy. He's here. Wait a sec."

She turned to me and handed me Mr. Yawkey's phone.

"Murph? Yeah! She's with me. Yeah! Okay. We'll be right there." I hung up. "Let's go, doll. You come along too, Tom. Half this case may be solved."

We took a cab the Charlestown Navy Yard located on the Boston side of the Mystic River. The yard was slowly becoming a ghost town since the end of the war. I let Tom pay the cabby and joined Detective Murphy and several squad cars at the end of a short, rickety wooden pier.

"Hi guys," Detective Murphy greeted. "All I need is an ID. We got this stiff who's been fish food for probably a week. Someone shooed him with cement and put him under this pier probably when the tide was out. Left the poor slob to watch himself drown. No identification on the victim. Not even any hints."

I could feel Penny shuddering at my side. I put my arm around her shoulder and pulled her close. "Let's go look. I've only seen a picture of Majors. You've seen all of him."

She looked at me, frowned, and then punched me in the arm - hard.

"Sorry! I didn't mean it that way. I just meant - well, you know what I meant."

"You don't have to look if you don't want to," Mr. Yawkey said. "If it's him, I'll recognize the face."

Murphy put out his hand, palm up. "Not this guy's face you won't."

"Why not?" Mr. Yawkey asked. "I discovered the guy and signed him to a contract."

Murphy shrugged! "You'll see." He led us off the pier, down a steep embankment and onto a small rocky beach. We walked under the pier to where the police had chipped the cement block away from the dead man's feet. He lay on a stretcher - covered by a sheet.

"Okay, pull the blanket back," Murphy instructed a uniformed officer.

The officer obeyed.

"What do you think, lady? Recognize him? Or what's left of him?"

Penny covered her mouth, gasped and almost vomited. The corpse had no eyeballs or nose - apparently eaten away by fish.

"I - I can't tell. He - he doesn't look human."

"Take it easy, Mam," Murphy said. "Does he have any identifying marks? You know, like a mole, scar, or tattoo?"

Penny pulled away from me and stared out into the harbor. The tide headed in and everyone's nasal passages were filled with the aroma of salt and fish. "He - he had a tattoo," she finally murmured.

One of the anxious reporters pushed his way in front of Penny. "What's your name, doll? I'm from the Globe."

It was 1946 and there were seven dailies in the city. I knew that Mr. Yawkey wouldn't be happy if even one of them printed a story about Majors. Murphy grabbed the man by the collar and roughly pulled him back. "Be human, will ya Mac? This may be the lady's husband." Murphy turned to Penny and whispered, "Where?"

"Stomach! One of those snake things that looks like a belt. It goes all the way around his waist."

Murphy slowly lifted the sheet, pulled up the man's soiled shirt, and slid down his pants.

Murphy and I gasped, locked eyes and nodded. Mr. Yawkey choked-up and turned away.

The reporter burst onto the scene again. "Is that your husband, lady? Is it? Is it? What's your name, lady? The public has a right to know." He snapped a picture of Penny standing near the dismembered dead body.

I roughly grabbed the man's collar. "Leave her alone, buddy, or you'll be reading your own name in the paper tomorrow. The obit page!" I then grabbed the camera and flung it far out into the murky harbor.

"You prick," the reporter yelled. "You can't do that. This is a free country. Freedom of the Press, you know. The public has a right to know about this. I'm just doing my job. I'm suing!"

Murphy, his red face beginning to resemble his red hair, pushed the reporter up against a large rock. "You're not suing anyone, asshole," he growled. "And if I read anything about this in tomorrow morning's edition, you'll be looking for a new job – in purgatory."

I led Penny and Mr. Yawkey back to the pier and placed them inside one of the squad cars. I then chatted with Murphy for a few minutes before joining them. We were driven back to Mr. Yawkey's office - Penny shivering all the way. "Sorry you had to go through that ordeal," I said when we were safely inside.

The team owner poured three brandies, gave away two and downed his with one big swallow. "I guess I was right about someone knocking off my great rookie," he said. "Now all we have to do is find out which one of my boys did it."

Penny still shook, but daintily sipped and said, "What kind of person would do that to another human being? Majors was a creep, but did he deserve that kind of treatment?"

"I've seen it before," I admitted. "Somehow Majors got the wrong people mad at him." I sent my attention to the boss. "And I'm beginning to wonder if maybe none of your boys knocked Majors off. I've met most of them and they all seem like good eggs. Except Higgins, of course! He has the persona to probably rub somebody out."

Mr. Yawkey smiled and shook his head. "Not Michael! He's a lot of things – bigot – drunk – asshole - but I know him too well. You drink with a guy enough times you get to really know him. Yup! Trust me! You can cross Mike off your list. When he retires I'm going to make him manager."

"Okay with me," I said, and then suddenly thinking that maybe? *No way! Mr. Yawkey and Higgins? No way! But just maybe!* "One less suspect for me to worry about," I said – maybe more to myself than to the boss. *The kid let Multimillionaire Mr. Yawkey down. Insulted him! He's a powerful rich guy. How dare anyone let him down?*

I had to change my mind, so - "Hey guys, do you know what a hit man is?"

Penny sipped her drink and shrugged. "A pinch hitter?"

I chuckled! "Not quite! It's not a baseball term. It's a gangster term for a guy who makes his living killing people."

"And?" That was Mr. Yawkey asking. "I've heard that a professional one can be hired for as little as a hundred dollars. I'm glad that I never hated anyone so much that I wished them dead. On the other hand, if I could find one to knock off the Yankees."

Thou dost protest too much. Those five famous Shakespeare words were the only ones I recall from grade school. Why? Because sometimes they reveal the perpetrator of a crime. I was taught that in Police School.

Penny creased her brow. "I wasn't brought up that way. I was taught that hate is a wasted emotion, and that a happy life was made up of three words."

"Yeah? What three words?" her boss asked.

"Give, forgive, and live."

I pondered the concept. "Makes sense! Give, forgive, and live. Yeah! I'll try and remember that. But there's a whole world full of people who don't follow those three ideas. And, if you did want someone put to sleep, and knew the right telephone number, it would be easy."

"And you think that's what happened to Majors?" Mr. Yawkey asked.

"Maybe! I don't know yet. We do know that he was messing in the drug world that could lead to disaster. I'm afraid that I'll have to check a few more sources other than the ball players."

Penny and Mr. Yawkey both cocked their eyebrows. "Are you really suggesting that maybe someone other than one of my players may be guilty?" the team's owner said. "Actually, that would be a relief."

"Birds of a feather flock together," I reminded everyone. "Drugs may be involved. That grenade thing smells like a professional. I don't think many of your players carry grenades, even though many of them served in the Armed Forces. The ones I've met face to face appear quite harmless. Let me make a phone call. I think I know someone who is familiar with the underworld. As I said, we may be looking in the wrong places. Let me use Penny's phone. This next call will have to be very private."

I excused myself, went into the front office, sat at Penny's desk and dialed.

I waited!

Someone picked up!

"Hello! It's Johnny. Ever heard of a Steve Majors - a doper rookie baseball player?"

The voice belonged to Wayne Mitchell, a lawyer who was employed by a retired judge. He played on my Park League team and was one of the nicest, kindest people I had ever met. Our team was sort of an honor-society thing. When a guy joined up he actually made a small cut on his thumb and rubbed it on the thumb of another player. Sounds foolish, but? Sort of like the Masons who swear life-time secrecy, and I've been told that at least half the presidents of the United States were Masons – so they can't be all that bad.

Wayne hesitated, avoided the question, and then congratulated me for making the Red Sox team – a dream of all semi-pro players. "I'll check on it for you. And we miss your Sunday bat."

I hung up and returned to Mr. Yawkey's office. "My friend will check it out and get back to me."

Mr. Yawkey stood up, stretched and announced, "I'm going to the men's room. You two behave yourselves while I'm gone. Okay?"

We both nodded, and when he was gone I pulled my chair next to Penny's. I took her hand in mine and asked, "Ever heard about the shell-part theory?"

"Not that I recall. What are shell parts?"

"When you walk along a beach you see lots of sea shells. Right?"

She agreed with a smile and eyebrow lift.

I said, "Somewhere on that beach, or in the water, is the other part of the shell - an identical fit."

"Never thought of that."

I attempted to divert my eye-attention away from her bust line, as it seemed to be trying to break through the fabric. "If you searched for the match you'd probably never find it. But we all know it's there - somewhere. Same is true with people. You're a shell part, and the other piece is somewhere. You may someday be lucky enough to find it - or not." I gently ran my fingers through her hair. "What do you think?"

She perked up, her eyes widened. "Are you describing a soul mate?"

"Yeah! Something like that! Most people spend a lifetime getting married, divorced, have affairs, one-night stands - all searching, searching, searching. But few ever find the other part that really fits. Then again, like on the beach, one day you look down and there it is - the matching shell part."

"I think you're flirting with me Mr. Dark. I'm engaged, you know." She squeezed my hand tightly.

I squeezed back, dropped her hand and got up. "I have a game to play. Afterwards, you and I will get you settled in my houseboat. You'll like it if you don't get seasick. The water glasses have white caps at breakfast."

CHAPTER ELEVEN

BOSTON POST HEADLINES 1946

1ST ELECTRIC BLANKET MANUFACTURED

JOHN F. KENNEDY ELECTED TO HOUSE OF REPRESENTITIVES

IN THE RED SOX DUGOUT THE LINEUP HAD BEEN POSTED for the afternoon game against the St. Louis Browns. DiMaggio was leading off. Pesky batted second. Williams third. York fourth. Doerr fifth. Wally Moses, a newly acquired ancient outfielder, but good hitter batted sixth. Higgins seventh. Partee eighth, and left handed pitcher Mickey Harris ninth. It was my job to find out if any of the other players had it in for Majors, although I now thought otherwise. The fact that Majors was a druggy suggested new suspects – ones that knew the killing business and not how to hit and field. And then I could never forget some of my father's clichés that always remain true. When you are looking for something, first check right under your nose. Even in my simple PI practice when I get hired to investigate a husband who might be cheating on his wife – or the other way around, I first look right under the nose. A neighbor, a secretary, even a relative. And with the wives, often it is the guy who drops by during the day while the husband is at work. The iceman, the bread man, the cleaning man, the plumber, etc. So in this case, who's right under my nose? Mr. Yawkey? Penny? Rudy?

Everyone stopped and stared - even the other team when Ted Williams strode into the cage, took a few practice swings, and then motioned to the pitcher to throw. He launched several over the right field fence - one into the center field bleachers, and two into the left field screen. Most fans agreed it was worth the price of admission just to watch Ted Williams practice. Some even admitted that they felt a chill run up and down their spine. It's called charisma.

I was the next batter and passed the tall, lanky left-hander as he stepped out of the cage. "Remember what I told you about your elbow," Ted said and smiled.

I felt a chill ride up and down my spine. *Ted Williams spoke to me again. Hot damn!*

I took a few practice swings and motioned to the pitcher to throw. The first ball came right down the shoot and I smashed it off the left field wall. I then proceeded to do that several more times. Manager Cronin took notice, said something to one of the coaches, and smiled. When I was finished, Johnny Pesky, the three hundred hitting shortstop patted me on the back. "Nice show, rookie," he said. "You'll be starting in right field before you know it. Where'd you say you played last year?"

I mumbled under my breath, "The Boston Park League."

The Red Sox beat up on the Brownies for the second straight game, 12-3. Williams, York and Higgins connected for homers, and Ted chipped in with three other hits. I was thrilled to just sit and watch in what I deemed the best seats in the ballpark. And they were free.

Tex Hughson, the scheduled starting pitcher for the next day sat in the dugout beside me when the game got underway. It gave us a chance to discuss baseball, and other topics. I was being paid to investigate – so I had better investigate.

"Whatever happened to that kid who struck out 27 batters in the Industrial League last year?" I asked, baiting my P.I. hook. "I heard you guys had signed him to a contract."

Somehow Mr. Yawkey had kept the murder story out of the newspapers at least for one day.

Hughson cringed. "That little prick? I don't know, and I don't care. We don't need him anyway. We're already way ahead in the standings."

"Rudy said Majors was a real ladies man. What do you think?"

Hughson covered his mouth and leaned close to my ear. "I'll tell you what I think about the punk. He's hooked on dope and he's a sick gambler. Neither fits in the big leagues."

I pondered the new information and what it might mean. *Majors a gambler?* "It's none of my business, but Rudy told me you caught Majors with your girlfriend?"

Hughson bit off a wad of tobacco and began to chaw. "Want a bite?"

I shook my head. "I got enough vices already. I smoke cigarettes, drink beer, and shoot darts. It's none of my business, but tell me about when you caught Majors with your girlfriend."

My cop father had taught me that if you preface a question with the words "Hey, it's none of my business, but ---." The questionee will usually spill the beans.

Hughson fooled me and didn't answer right way. He furrowed his brow and chawed rapidly, stared into my eyes and cracked a smile. "I got a chance to win twenty this year," he said. "Coulda won twenty in '44, but got screwed. Got drafted in September."

"Do you still have the same girlfriend you had in Spring Training?"

"You're a nosy son-of-bitch, aint'cha."

I forced a friendly smile. "Just making idle conversation."

Hughson spat some tobacco juice out onto the field in front of the dugout.

"I guess I'll have to learn how to do that," I said. "And also scratch my balls."

Hughson relaxed and laughed. "You got Moxie, kid. I lost my temper when I caught Majors with my gal. I think it was more at her. I think she liked him. He's a handsome cuss. I punched him a few times. Not with my pitching hand though. I'm too smart for that."

"Any idea where he is? I never met him yet."

"I don't know, and care less. What the hell do you care for?"

I slid a seat away from the big left-handed pitcher. "Just making conversation. I heard that everyone hates Majors, and I wondered why. That's all." Hughson had opened more than most people. He was no longer a suspect. And for the rest of the afternoon I chatted with most of the players - short and too the point. None of them asked for a lawyer or wanted to see a warrant and they pretty much all opened up quite easily.

After the game and we were all showering in the locker room, Williams asked Manager Cronin why he didn't let the rookie pinch hit. "He coulda batted for me," Ted said. "I'm not greedy. If we're ahead tomorrow, let the kid take a lick."

A few of the other players nodded in agreement. I figured that Cronin probably knew the whole story about my cover and wasn't about to let a gimpy kneed private eye play in a Big League game. But, on the other hand, that was the cover, and it would be even a better cover if Cronin let me into a few games. He could always use a pinch runner if I was lucky enough to get a hit. I started to shake all over just thinking about it. *Maybe I'll get to bat tomorrow. Maybe I'll piss my wool baseball pants right in front of twenty thousand fans.*

As we were leaving the locker-room I told Rudy about my plans to move Penny into my houseboat with old Uncle Bill. The story would be that she'd broken up with Nash and taken a liking to the rookie. *Hey, that's me!*

Rudy couldn't stop laughing. "I still don't think you're old enough to know about the birds and the bees. That thing between your legs? You know how to use it? And Penny's only twenty something. She may still be a virgin. My mother caught me in the bathtub once playing with myself. I was so embarrassed I said something like - I was only cleaning it, mother, and then it went off."

I chuckled at the big Indian's joke. Or maybe it wasn't a joke. "I'll remember that one if Penny catches me in the bathtub."

An hour later Penny and I were climbing out of a cab on Atlantic Avenue next to Boston Harbor. I got out first and allowed my eyes to circuit the area. Everything appeared natural. No bombers with grenades in sight, or strange looking cars - whatever a strange looking car would look like hiding a bomber with a grenade. We walked to the end of a long wooden dock. Several large but empty fishing boats were tied to both sides of the pier. Looming up in the fog was a small, faded white houseboat, maybe fifty feet long and thirty feet wide. The barge was one and a half stories consisting of a few rooms with a deck on the first floor, and another smaller room on top. A tiny lamp illuminated the front door, along with a sign reading: BEWARE, ATTACK DOG ON PREMISES.

"I'm afraid of dogs," Penny said and stepped back.

I chuckled. "We don't have a dog - just a sign. It works just as well, and we don't have to feed it."

I opened the front door and ushered Penny inside.

"This is great, Sir Lancelot," she giggled and perused the room. "I always wanted my own private knight to guard me. Nash once fitted me for a chastity belt before he went out of town."

I got a laugh out of that one, imagining myself trying to pick the lock with a bobby pin. I flipped my hat and coat onto a corner rack and helped Penny off with her jacket. "There's a small bedroom upstairs that you can have," I said. "Good view of the harbor. Bill sleeps down the hall, and I'll take this couch. Not much space on this tug, but enough for two bachelors who are never home."

Penny wandered around the nautical decorated room. The windows were shaped like portholes. Fisherman's nets hung from the ceiling, and the wooden walls were Navy gray - knotty pine. "Looks comfy," she said. "You do the interior decorating?"

"My uncle was Navy in WW1. He loves the salt water. This is as close as he could get without renting a submarine."

She studied some framed pictures covering one entire wall. "Who's this little kid in a baseball uniform?"

"That's always been my passion," I said and walked over and stood beside her. "That picture was taken in fifth grade." I then pointed to a picture of a handsome smiling man wearing a police uniform. "That's my dad. He was my best friend."

"He died when you were?"

"Eleven!"

"From?"

"He was a good cop and forgot to shoot first and say stick 'em up second!"

"What about your mother?"

I pointed to an old grainy snapshot - a wedding picture. My mother wore a wide smile, was short, pretty and skinny. "After my father's death she went away and drowned herself in alcohol. I came here to live with Uncle Bill."

Penny looked at the other photos while I made two drinks - gin and tonics. She noticed my cork dartboard hanging beside the photo gallery. "I can do that sport."

"Uncle Bill and I shoot for dimes," I said. "I let him win sometimes."

I sat down on a long fake leather couch and waved for her to join me. "On a more serious note," I began, "what happens when Nash finds out where you've gone?"

"He called the office today. Mr. Yawkey clued him in."

"And what was his alibi for not being at the Waldorf?"

"He stayed with a friend instead. Cheaper! Made sense to me. Why? Do you think he's lying? Obviously Mr. Yawkey doesn't like him. My boss is very protective of me. Like a surrogate father."

"I want you to tell me about everyone who's been in your apartment during the past eight months."

Penny scowled. "Are you nuts? How can I remember that?"

I moved one cushion closer and gently grabbed her arm. "Because you have to. I told you that I think that whoever threw that grenade knew that your apartment was on the right side of the building. He wouldn't have taken a chance at guessing - so he must have known."

Penny took The Thinker pose, and then said, "The real estate agent was a man - and kinda cute. I flirted a little - but only a tad. He even asked me out on a date. I said no. But he seemed quite harmless. He invited me to the Totem Pole Ballroom in Newton. Ever been there? They get the big bands. Serve no booze."

"I've taken dates there. Great big soft couches with high backs. Swell for making out if you're a teenager. I'd take you there if you wanted." I didn't know why I said that. "Now if you don't mind, tell me about anyone else who's been in your apartment."

Penny changed positions, moved a cushion closer so our legs were touching. "Nash invited a few gentlemen for dinner one night - maybe a week ago. I don't know any of them, and never laid eyes on any of them again."

"Did they talk about bonds?"

"Not in front of me."

I remembered seeing an intercom on Penny's living room desk. *I wonder if there's one like it in her bedroom?* "But you know what they talked about when you weren't in the room!"

Penny looked down, like ashamed. "Yeah, I do. I listened."

"Want to tell me about it? What does your fiancée really do for a living?"

She hesitated, fidgeted with her fingernails, and began tapping them on my thick wooden coffee table shaped like a whale. She looked me straight in the eyes. "He's a high-class bookie."

"What's the difference between high-class and low-class? They're both against the law."

"Silly law I think. People like to bet, and should be able to bet, and then pretty much do anything they want to do - if it doesn't infringe on somebody else's freedom in a free country. They allow Bingo at the Catholic Church every Wednesday night. Isn't that gambling?"

"Different," I said, really knowing that it wasn't different. "I agree that people should be able to make bets, but unfortunately lots of gamblers go broke, lose their houses, their families, and who knows what else. And the bad bookies beat the shit out of people who don't pay. But you say he's a high-class bookie? They probably don't break legs and arms - just a person's heart."

Her stare became a glare. "He's a nice man. He wouldn't hurt a fly."

"Sorry, sorry! I've never even met the man. But let's just say that maybe he got in a little deep and was threatened - pay up or your girlfriend gets it? Something like that! How would he react? Hightail it out of town - maybe?"

"Boy, are you grasping at straws, Johnny. He wouldn't let anything bad happen to me. I know him. Heck, we're going to get married."

I felt that remark stab me deep in my chest. "Look Penny, people don't do things for no reason. There always has to be a motive. Sometimes in crime-work, once you discover the motive, it's easy to discover the culprit. Have you ever heard him suggest that he might be in trouble?"

She shrugged!

"And what were the nationalities of his guests that night?"

She glared again. "Why? What difference does that make? Are you a bigot? If they were Italian that means he's in with the Mafia? If they were Jews that means they should be imprisoned at Auschwitz?"

"Something like that! But not the Jewish part, of course. Do you recall any of the last names?"

Penny scratched her permed hairdo. "How about Catalano? Yeah, one of the bigger men was Mr. Catalano. Then another one, a small mousy guy - his name was - um - Rizzo. Yeah, Rizzo! The third man was big and never talked. So I never got his name."

"And they talked about bookmaking?"

"Uh, huh! Until I got bored, so I turned off the intercom and listened to the radio. The Lux Radio Theater. They do movies every week. That night they did..."

"Yeah, yeah, I know the show. Let's get back to Nash and his cronies. Did you overhear anything juicy?"

She cuddled close to me, fluttered her eyelashes and purred. "Look Johnny, I heard some real scandalous tidbits, but I don't want to see Nash get into any trouble. Your job is to find out who murdered Steve Majors - and now to protect me. I'll tell you about what they were planning if you promise not to act on it."

I pulled away and nodded. "I'm not a cop, Penny. I can't arrest anyone. Now please tell me what they were planning."

"A fixed horse race at Narraganset Park in Rhode Island this Saturday. Ever been to the races, Johnny?"

"Too many times. My uncle makes me take him every weekend so he can visit his money. Tell me about this fixed race."

"Well, they know this trainer who has a string of horses in New York and New England. He'll take a horse and stiff him maybe five or six times over a few month period, and then drop him into an easy spot where they know the horse can't lose. In other words, the horse is a legitimate ten or fifteen thousand-dollar horse. They run him for the fifteen. He loses badly. They run him for ten, and he loses badly. Then they drop him to the bottom and he still loses badly. You see what they are setting up?"

I nodded! I could see! I knew that 90% of all horses racing in the country are cheap and run in what's called Claiming Races. That means that someone else can buy the horse right out of the race. In other words, if you are the owner and don't want to lose the horse, you run him against like competitive company.

Penny said, "Nash has taken me to Suffolk Downs a few times. The last visit he bet on some awful looking nag that won and paid fifty dollars. Do you think it was a setup?"

"You tell me!"

"It was!"

"So I assume that the real reason he was in New York was to bet a horse?"

"Right!"

"When is he expected back in town?"

"Tonight!"

"And when's that Narraganset race?"

"Saturday."

"Damn! I have a ballgame."

"Can't you get sick? Hurt your knee, or something?"

"Or something! Yeah! I'll think of something. I still think that when you lay down with horses you get up with manure."

"Isn't that shit?"

"I don't talk like that in front of a lady."

Penny glanced around the room and smiled. "Who came in?"

"Can you get Nash to invite us to the races on Saturday?" I asked, not feeling humorous. "Maybe we can meet some of his boys and draw our own conclusions. I'm telling you right now, he's running with a tough crowd."

"Not too tough for my Lancelot, I bet," Penny said and poked me on the arm. Not too hard.

"Ouch! That hurt!" I finished off my drink. "Hey, I have a new scene that might allow you to sleep better at night."

"What's that, Johnny?" she purred. "I like scenes, especially if you're in them."

"It's none of my business, but how many nights a week does Nash spend in your apartment?"

She pulled away and wrinkled her brow. "Johnny, what kind of a girl do you think I am?"

"I don't get paid to judge people, doll. Just answer my question."

"Well, if you must know, maybe two or three. But, believe it or not, I'm still a virgin."

"Then that could be it?" I said and rubbed my hands together.

"What's it?"

"It's a long shot, but how about this? Nash was the intended victim, not you. The bomber saw you with a man, who was me, and thought it was Nash."

Penny pursed her lips like Gene Tierney. "That would put me out of danger, wouldn't it?"

"But it puts Nash in constant danger. Do you think he'll cooperate?"

"In what way?"

"Stay away from you until we finish filling in the blanks of this crossword puzzle."

"I don't know. How would I know? The only thing he seems to respond to is money. Maybe Mr. Yawkey would make a donation - or something."

CHAPTER TWELVE

BOSTON POST HEADLINES 1946

MOSLEMS HINDUS RIOT IN CALCUTTA 4000 KILLED

NAT. BASKETBALL ASSN. FORMED IN NYC

PENNY AND I STIFFENED WHEN WE HEARD the front door open. I moved Penny's head off my lap, stood up and spun around - a nine-inch knife in my hand.

Donald Nash loomed just inside the doorway carrying a large arrangement of red roses. He wasn't smiling. Yesterday I had received a bio from Murphy. Donald Nash, a bookie, who claimed to be a bond salesman was born in Revere, Massachusetts 1910. His parents ran a concession stand at the large beach area amusement park. Nash learned the business, eventually owning several games designed to fleece the crowd of many dollars before awarding a cheap kewpie doll. The dolls cost a dollar apiece. No one wins until the game has realized ten bucks. In the mid thirties he began hanging around the new Suffolk Downs Race Track, eventually learning how to be a tout. That means that if there are eight horses in a race, the tout approaches eight people, tells them that he has a hot tip. He gives each of them a different winner and insists that when they bet they bet ten bucks for him. Of course, the tout has at least one winner every time, and only revisits that lucky customer after the race to collect his winnings. PS - He then has to avoid the other seven suckers. And soon outlives his welcome and has to find another track. Nash became a successful, well-dressed bookie.

"You won't need that knife, buddy," Nash muttered. "You must be Dark."

I kept my eyes on the intruder and asked Penny," Is that who I think it is?"

"It's him," she said, got up and walked over to Nash, throwing her arms around his bulky form. "Hi, dear. Missed you a lot. Did you bring me a present other than the flowers?"

He smiled and kissed her lips, hard. "Later! Now let's get outta this joint. I don't like this place. Smells like fish."

I sat back down on the couch and winced.

Penny hesitantly stepped back. "I don't know. Didn't you hear what happened at my apartment? I don't think it's safe."

He handed her a small package. It brought an instant beam to her face. She unwrapped it, blinked and smiled. It was an expensive shiny diamond broach. She threw her arms around Nash's neck. He flashed a sly grin at me and proceeded to attach the broach to her blouse, close to her left breast - touching it - by mistake, of course.

She giggled.

I felt heat around my collar. *Why the hell am I so jealous? I asked myself. This bird is the dame's fiancée. He certainly has every right to give her an expensive present. And, he has a right to touch her tits. Doesn't he?*

I then put out a hand to Nash, who took it and shook. "I guess Mr. Yawkey told you what Penny's doing here. I get paid to protect people, and I don't want you to get the wrong idea."

Nash nodded, put a Camel cigarette between his lips and sat down beside Penny on my couch. He gave her a book of matches and said, "Match it honey."

She obeyed!

He was younger looking than his forty plus years, in athletic shape, like a football fullback, slicked back brown hair, cleanly shaven, and thin slits for eyes. His black, three-piece expensive looking suit sported pin stripes. To me, he resembled the epitome of a con man, or a lawyer. *Same difference,* I thought.

"She doesn't have to stay here now that I'm here, Mr. Dick," Nash said. "But thanks for taking care of her while I was gone on my business trip."

I shot a questioning glance at Penny. *Shall I let her go?* I asked myself. *No way! Mr. Yawkey is paying me to take care of her.*

"It's Dark, Mr. Nash." I said and held my cool, and my seat. "Jonathan Dark, Private Detective! I even have a license to do what I do. And you never told us if you heard about the bombing?"

Nash frowned. "I heard and that's why I'm here. As a matter of fact, I'm not sure that Penny wouldn't be safer at my house."

He looked at me through squinted eyes. "How the hell do I know that the bombers weren't trying to blow you up?"

Penny finally got up enough courage to put in her two cents. "I - I've been told to stay here." she stuttered.

"By who?" Nash asked, arrogantly. "I think I know what's best for my fiancé."

I clenched my fist, but held my poise. I had once taken a course in high school that stuck in my memory and helped immensely in my chosen field. It was the only course I could recall scoring a grade of better than a D. Psychology 101. It taught how to climb into another person's head and look through their eyes. I remembered the teacher telling the half-asleep students, "You already know what you think about things, and most people don't give a damn what the other person is thinking. So, if you want to excel in life, analyze what the other person is thinking and deal from their side of the table. It will always give you the edge. I had always tried to follow that suggestion. I could now empathize with Nash's position. *The poor prick!*

"Mr. Yawkey hired me to watch out for his secretary," I calmly said. "I can understand how you feel, and I'm terribly sorry. By the way, is there any chance that the bomber was after you?"

Nash began to laugh. "Me? Why me? I sell bonds for a living. And not War Bonds."

I shook my head. "Why don't we all level with each other, Mr. Nash? I'm pretending to be a ballplayer in order to find out what happened to Steve Majors. You're posing as a bond salesman when we all know that you're a bookie."

Nash kept his features calm and composed. "Who told you that?" He looked at Penny. "Did your snot nosed brother tell you that I'm a bookie, dear?"

"No! And he's not snot nosed," Penny said and became agitated at Nash's verbal attack on a member of her family. I had also learned that fact in Psychology 101. You don't ever put down someone else's family member - no matter how bad they are. It just don't cut it!

Penny angrily removed the broach and flipped it onto Nash's lap, and then ran down the hall - out of sight, slamming a door loudly behind her. I wanted to smile and applaud – but held my cool.

Nash forced a grin. "Women! They're all the same. You can't live with 'em, and you can't shoot 'em."

I didn't laugh at the crude man's attempt at humor. "Maybe you shouldn't be so naive, Mr. Nash. How long did you think you could fool her?"

"As long as I wanted to, Mr. Dork," Nash grunted. "I'm accustomed to getting what I want."

I fumbled in my coat pocket for a cigarette, found a loose Chesterfield, lit it, and blew a nice round smoke ring. I then watched it slowly float to the ceiling and disappear in its own magic way into the fishnets. It was there for a split second - then poof, and then gone. I was good at more than just throwing darts.

"By any chance are you planning to go to Narraganset on Saturday?" I asked, already knowing the answer. "By the way, my name's Dark. D A R K."

Nash frowned, seeming to be finally losing his cool. "Not that it's any of your fucking business, but yes. I try to go to the track every Saturday."

"My uncle would love you," I said. "He's a loyal fan of the ponies. Would you mind if we went with you?"

Nash answered abruptly. "I would mind. I don't even know you or your uncle."

"I'll go too," Penny said, bouncing back down the hall. "I like the horses." She was holding a small pair of nail clippers, picked up the broach, and clipped off the price tag.

"We'll talk about it in the morning," Nash said, irately. "I'm tired and I'm going home." He turned to Penny and said with composure, "Coming, dear?"

Penny's lips went thin. "I don't think I'd be comfortable doing that, Donny. You go along and I'll see you in the morning. By the way, thanks for the broach. Must have been expensive."

I chuckled to myself. It was easy to climb into her mind. She had been eavesdropping from the bathroom.

Nash made a disagreeable face. "If Mr. Yawkey is paying Dork to be a bodyguard, I guess he has to go to the races if you go." He grabbed his coat and hat, kissed Penny quickly on the cheek, and made a hurried departure.

"He can be a jerk," Penny said. "Sorry! You didn't deserve that treatment. Want to shoot some darts?"

We spent the next hour shooting darts, drinking brandy, and getting inebriated. I allowed her to win every game.

"You smink! Oopsy! I mean you stink at this sport," she slurred. "What were you going to do with that nine-inch knife if the intruder was a bad man?"

"Part his hair," I said, and then flipped a dart over my head with my back to the board.
Bulls-eye!

CHAPTER THIRTEEN

BOSTON POST HEADLINES 1946

PRESIDENT TRUMAN CREATES CIA

PATENT FILED IN US FOR A-BOMBS

THE NEXT MORNING I AWOKE TO THE SMELL of sizzling bacon. I showered and found a fresh white shirt and a neat bow tie. It was a red clip-on. *Was I trying to impress someone?*

I exited the bathroom and addressed Penny who was cooking. "Did you meet my uncle?"

"Never saw him. Did he come home yet?"

"At about one. I told him about Nash. He's all excited about going to Narraganset on Saturday."

The phone rang. I answered, listened, and then turned to Penny. "It's someone named Butch. Your brother?"

She nodded and took the phone. Chatted for a minute, and then asked me, "Can he come for breakfast? He must have gotten your number from Nash. I hope that's okay."

I nodded. "Invite him over. I'd like to meet him."

It was close to nine o'clock. The Fenway office didn't open until eleven. I dialed Mr. Yawkey's Ritz Carlton telephone number. The boss stayed at the exclusive hotel when in Boston during the Red Sox home games. Penny received a full-time secretary's salary for part-time hours - a plush job.

Mr. Yawkey came to the phone. "Looks like we're going to win it all this year, son. I really can't get over seeing Majors like that. Damn! I've never seen a dead body. How's the detective work going?"

I cupped my hand over the mouthpiece so Penny couldn't listen in. "You were right about Majors being murdered, sir. But so far - no clues! It does look like a professional job to me and that should give you some relief. It exonerates any of your boys."

"So who the hell else from around here even knew this kid?"

"It doesn't take druggies very long to link up when they move to a new town, sir. And when you mess with dope, you end up hanging with the wrong crowd. I'm sure that's what happened to Majors."

"Do you think Penny's life might still be in danger," Mr. Yawkey asked. "Good secretaries are hard to find - especially smart pretty ones. And Penny is a smart pretty one."

"I met Nash last night," I said. "I don't think he's too happy with this arrangement, and I don't think he likes me. I checked with the cops, and while Nashy has no record, he does hang with a known bookmaker who does have a record. Nash is pretty smooth - and I can see why Penny took a liking to him. He gives her expensive gifts. Very expensive! And while he's built like an athlete I'm sure the only sport he ever played was with a pool stick - if you want to call that a sport. To answer your question, as long as she's linked to him she could be in danger."

"Well, I guess that's another reason that I should keep you on the payroll - at least to guard her and clean up this mess. What do you think?"

I caught the sounds an ice tinkling on glass. Mr. Yawkey was a morning drinker. "Look Sir, I mean Tom, I know you've been through a lot lately. It isn't often that one of your ballplayers takes a cement-shoe swim in Boston Harbor. And I know you'd never forgive yourself if anything happened to Penny. Why don't you go to your South Carolina estate for a week and let me work things out around here? Just a week! That'll give me enough time to hopefully get Nash out of Penny's life and find out who killed Majors. I'll work with detective Murphy to keep all of those nosy reporters away. Whaddya say, Tom?"

I heard more tinkling, a long sigh, and then, "Okay, son. You talked me into it. Ever thought about being a salesman? You're pretty good at it. Penny has my South Carolina telephone number. And it is actually a good time for me to revisit. My wife and I had planned to stay there for a few weeks until the Majors' mess. She's still down there."

"Revisit? When were you last there, sir?"

"The week Majors joined the team Mrs. Yawkey and I flew to South Carolina. I flew back the day before my meeting with you. Why do you ask?"

I guess I can cross Mr. Yawkey off my suspect list, I told myself. "I, um - I was just curious. I'm sure it's very nice there this time of year."

"Hot!" he said. "But my wife likes the seclusion of the farm. You'll have to meet her someday. She was once a model. Very hot!"

We both hung up. I smiled at Penny, and we started eating our breakfast. "Mr. Yawkey is going to his home in South Carolina for a week. That should give you a well-needed rest."

"Does he still think one of the players killed Majors?"

"No way! My money now says that Majors was a dope addict and somehow got involved with the wrong crowd."

"What are you going to do next?"

"Keep playing ball, and then attend the races at Narragansett on Saturday with you, dear. What do you usually do when Mr. Yawkey leaves town?"

"I answer the phone, tidy things up, and go home early - or go to the game. Why?"

"I guess we should attend that new Humphrey movie and find out how real gumshoes solve crimes in 90 minutes - at least in Hollywood."

The front door burst open. I grabbed my knife. Penny chopped at my arm. "It's only my brother, Butch. He's harmless."

I had no bios on Butch so would have to draw my own conclusions. Psychology 101 would help. I studied the boy. *Maybe twenty-five at the most. Tall, gangly with long stringy hair hanging to his collar. He looks like a wild sort. His numerous tattoos tell me that he might have spent some time in Reform School, or prison. Penny told me that she helps him when he's down and out. He recently began frequenting local racetracks. While he displays no visible means of support, his sister revealed that he sometimes waves cash around. I would deduce that he hangs with the wrong crowd. Drugs?*

Butch swiftly moved to his sister's side and gave her a big bear hug. "Hi, Sis. Understand you've had a bad time of it. I've been in Rhode Island and came as soon as I heard." He shot a poisonous glance at me. "Who's this joker? Want me to get rid of him?"

I stifled the urge to punch out the punk, but knew that wouldn't sit too well with Penny. She put an arm on my shoulder and pulled me close. "He's the man who saved my life, Butch, and this is his place. Mr. Yawkey hired him as a bodyguard."

The tall kid bowed and reached out to shake my hand. "Thanks, bud. Whaddaya do for a living?"

"Other people's laundry," I said through clenched teeth.

"He's a private detective," Penny said.

I held my cool, swearing to myself that I would break at least two noses before the caper was over – Butch and Nash. I took Penny's hand in mine and said, "We can all continue this sarcasm contest, or we can put our heads together and figure out who knocked off Steve Majors and threw a grenade into

Penny's window. What do you think, Butch? I humbly admit I could use the help."

Butch shrugged his shoulders, nibbled on some bacon, and finished off a piece of toast. "I didn't know Majors got killed. Never even met him. Hey, I got some business this morning. Maybe I'll see you guys at the game this afternoon." He looked at Penny. "Thanks for the breakfast Sis. Got any extra dough? I'm a little short this week. Worked real hard though, and of course I'll pay you back. I've been getting real unlucky at cards lately. But what goes down must come up. My luck is bound to change. Then I can pay you back all the dough that I owe you."

Penny didn't question him, fumbled in her purse, and came up with a ten. "Maybe you should think about getting a regular job, Butch. I don't think your gambling is ever going to amount to anything."

He grunted a few times, grabbed his jacket and headed for the door. "I figured a new system at the ponies. If it works, I'll be rich."

"Allow me to apologize for the rude actions of my brother," Penny said after he was gone. "You certainly didn't deserve that disrespectful treatment."

"I got thick skin," I lied.

"I love my brother," she said. "But I really don't know how to get him on the right track. I thought his friendship with Nash would help. But I think things are getting worse."

The phone rang. Penny answered, listened, and then handed the receiver to me.

I talked in a low tone for a few minutes, and then said something about meeting at the racetrack the next day, and hung up.

"That was my lawyer friend, Wayne Mitchell," I said. "He says Nash is on a list to be eliminated by people from out of town."

Penny's face froze. "How does he know that? Out of town? What does that mean?"

"It means that Nash is a guy you want to steer clear of. It means that most likely that grenade was meant for Nashy. Whoever was after him thought I was him that night."

"Do you think Nash knows that?"

I shrugged. "I don't know, but Nash is a tough cookie. You'll meet my lawyer friend tomorrow at the track."

"What does being a lawyer have to do with knowing stuff like who has a hit out for who?"

"Connections! He works for a judge – a former DA. Those people are forced to rub elbows with all types – good and bad."

"So how do you know Wayne?"

"He's a pitcher in the Park League. We play on the same team." *If I could only change the subject*, I wished.

And suddenly - "Who the hell is she?" a grumbling voice bellowed from the hall as a crusty old man wheeled himself into the main room. "She's cute enough, son. Is she a hooker, or your latest girl friend – or a little bit of both?"

I shook my head. "Sorry about that, Penny. When I talked to him late last night I didn't tell him about you. If I had he wouldn't have remembered anyway. And I don't hang with hookers."

She boldly walked over to the old man and shook his hand. "I'm Penny. I work for Mr. Yawkey of the Red Sox. I'm also your new tenant. Johnny tells me you're a war hero."

Uncle Bill poured himself some hot coffee and retrieved an orange from the icebox. He bit off the top and began sucking. His bio, actually not existing, would read like this: *William Atherton Dark was born in 1885 in Newton, Massachusetts, a small city about 10 miles West of Boston. He had one brother, Charles, 10 years younger. Bill starred on the Newton High School baseball team, played for Toronto in the minors, never quite making it to the big time. In 1915, at the age of 30, he went to Spring Training with the Red Sox, meeting and hanging around with a young rookie named George Herman Ruth, who made the team and became a star. A dejected Bill was sent back to the minors. But he and Ruth remained lifelong drinking buddies. In 1917, Billy Dark enlisted in the United States Navy, was sent to Europe and had a leg shot off. For the rest of his life he lived on a houseboat barge in Boston Harbor purchased for him by none other than Babe Ruth who had a hell of a time spending all the money he was making as an ace pitcher and power hitter. Bill received a small WWI pension. In 1935 Bill's brother, Charlie, a Boston cop who was Johnny's father was killed by a gangster's bullet. Charlie's wife never recovered from the shock and took to the bottle and loose men. Bill unofficially adopted Charlie's 11-year old son and raised him as his own. Bill was average height, very skinny, sported a Clark Gable mustache, wore thick bifocals, and was never seen without a black felt fedora.*

"He injects gin into the oranges," I whispered. "He'll be okay after a few sucks."

Penny's eyes widened. "Are you kidding? I had an orange last night before I went to sleep. Maybe that's why I have a headache. An orange hang over?"

CHAPTER FOURTEEN

BOSTON POST HEADLINES 1946

DODGERS HEAD NO-HITS BOSTON BRAVES

AL WINS 13TH ALL STAR GAME AT FENWAY PARK 12-0

THAT AFTERNOON PENNY WATCHED THE GAME from the safety of Mr. Yawkey's office as the Red Sox were now playing the hated New York Yankees led by Joltin' Joe DiMaggio. Dave Ferris, already a twenty game winner, gave up a three run homer in the first inning to DiMaggio.

I clapped a few times before noticing frowns from my fellow players. Mace Brown, the veteran relief pitcher was seated beside me and whispered, "We don't root for the opponents, kid. Joe is a nice guy, but he's the enemy. Sorry!"

I felt foolish, but took the opportunity to ask Brown about his tiff with Majors. Brown still had a bandage on his left hand from the altercation several months earlier. It was a good motive even though I was convinced that none of the players had committed the murder. But, on the other hand, I knew that hit men could be bought cheap and Brown was one of the few players I had not questioned.

"What's it feel like to play for a sure pennant winner?" I asked.

"Seen teams fold in September."

"These guys look pretty good to me," I said. "I certainly appreciate being here."

"Ditto!" he agreed. "I feel damn lucky to be playing with a bunch of great players. I've been with some pretty lousy teams."

"I understand that Majors throws a pretty mean fastball," I said and waited. The police had not released any information on the murder. And they really couldn't check on an orphan's family.

"That little prick?" Brown waved his still bandaged left hand in front of my nose. "No wonder he hasn't shown up for a week. He's afraid! He knows that I owe him one."

"And I understand that a few of the other players also owe him one or two."

Brown chuckled. "You're right about that."

Doerr was up and hit a fastball off the left field wall for a double. He was the fifth batter in the order. Old man Wally Moses followed.

"Rudy told me what happened to you in that barroom in Florida," I said. "I'm surprised you didn't retaliate right then."

Brown frowned. "I woulda, kid. But Rudy hustled Majors outta there so fast I didn't get a chance."

"Did you ever confront Majors again?"

"It was at the end of Spring Training and the Sox decided to hire a private doctor for the youngster. I understand that he's been in rehab most of the summer."

"When he recently rejoined the team did you notice any change?"

Brown didn't answer, just chawed on his tobacco and jumped up when Moses singled to left driving in Doerr with the first Sox run. He then turned to me and said, "You ask a lot of questions. You writing a book or something?"

"Just making polite conversation," I lied. "So you never got a chance to get your revenge?"

Brown unbuttoned the two top buttons of his wool shirt and revealed a chain with a Jesus cross hanging from it. "He's my savior," he said. "Vengeance be mine sayeth the Lord! So I figure that everyone gets what coming to them in this life – or least in the next. I'll let my savior take care of the revenge for me."

I slid my butt next to Eddie Pellagrini - the only local boy on the team and another one who I hadn't talked to yet. A good fielder and fair hitter, he had the misfortune to be playing behind Johnny Pesky. Pellagrini also served three years in the Navy. He has the distinction of hitting a home run his first time at bat in the league. No one will ever do it twice, so his record is safe.

"Like your swing, rookie," Pellagrini said with a smile. "Understand you're also a local boy."

"Newton! Ever play any local ball?"

"Dorchester High School in 1935 through 1937. When did you play?"

I counted on my fingers. "Newton High 1935 - 1938. Then I played in the Boston Park League. Still do." I hesitated. "I mean, still did until I made this team. Maybe we played against each other."

"Maybe! I'll probably end up in the Park League someday. I don't think I'm going to beat Pesky out for his job. Maybe they'll trade me next year and I'll get a better chance to play. I hate sitting on the bench."

Roy Partee flied out to end the Red Sox first inning.

"I hear that Spring Training was quite colorful with that Major's kid acting up," I said.

Pellagrini didn't answer, but patted Dave Ferris on his butt as he left the dugout for the second inning "He's a good pitcher," Pellagrini said.

"What about Majors? Will he be a big winner?"

Pellagrini turned to face me and displayed a creased brow. "You got a hard-on for this Majors kid? I don't think you'll ever see him pitch here, or for any other team. Not even in the Park League."

I double-taked. "I – I thought he had a great fastball."

Pellagrini nodded. "A fastball, fast mouth, and fast prick. The kid is his own worst enemy. He's a dope addict."

"Rudy said the kid was having some kind of rehab."

"He did! And he came back here last week. I went out with him a few nights and watched him in action. The first night he drank ginger ale and seemed to behave himself. The second night we found some dance place joint on Revere Beach. He started with ginger ale and ended up with a few whiskey shots. Then he started making too many visits to the bathroom. I've been around the block a few times and know what that can mean – and he didn't have the runs. After about an hour he was completely stoned. Then he hit on some cheap looking, over made-up dame with big jugs. He was showing off. He started bragging that he was a Red Sox pitcher and announced he could out-drink everyone in the room, and then proceeded to do it. I had to carry him out and take him home to Rudy."

"What happened to the girl with the big jugs?"

Pellagrini smiled. "I went back to the dance hall. I don't drink and I'm still single."

"Sounds like you were the only player on the team who befriended Majors. Is that right?"

Pellagrini didn't answer, got up and walked to the water cooler for a drink. *Did I strike a nerve?* I asked myself. The shortstop returned carrying a two chilled Coke bottles and handed one to me. "What do you know about dope?" he asked and sat down.

"My father was a cop," I answered. I decided not to tell him that I also spent two years on the force.

"Did he tell you about marijuana, heroin, and cocaine?"

"A little! Why?"

Pellagrini took a deep swallow of Coke from the bottle. "Did you know that at the turn of the century this was originally made with cocaine, and that's where the name came from?"

I shook my head. "That would explain its popularity."

"Majors was hooked on dope. That means he had to get it from somewhere."

"Makes sense to me, but so what?"

"He supposedly finished rehab in Florida and got a clean bill of health to rejoin the team two weeks ago."

"So?"

"So, within a few days he was stoned again. Rudy will tell you that."

"So the kid didn't kick the habit," I said. "He wouldn't be the first addict to have trouble kicking the habit."

"It also meant something else."

"What was that?"

"It would seem to me that getting hooked up with a drug dealer in a new city would take more than a few days," Pellagrini said. "What do you think?"

I hesitated, and then nodded my head. "So Majors was back doing drugs within forty-eight hours of his arrival in Boston. That tells me that his dealer is someone connected with the team - not necessarily a player. And most of the currant players are war veterans. So I suppose one could be on something."

Pellagrini nodded and said, "Hey, when you're sitting in a foxhole, or floating on a ship waiting to get shot, a little dope isn't something you debate about."

"I didn't serve," I humbly confessed. "I tried to sign up, but got rejected. Bad knee!"

Pellagrini turned his attention to Dom DiMaggio who singled up the middle. "Great hit," he yelled and clapped his hands.

"So if I wanted some dope I could spread the word around and someone connected to the club would sell it to me?" I whispered.

Pellagrini put his fingers to his lips. "Shh! I didn't say that Majors was getting his drugs from anyone on the team. I just think it's a coincidence that he hooked up with someone so fast. You know? Like someone who knows someone who knows someone."

"Got any ideas?"

"Shut up and watch Williams hit. You may learn something."

Ted had just strolled up the plate so I shut up and watched. Williams was famous for never swinging at anything not in the strike zone, and he even had the respect of many umpires who would never call a ball if the Splendid Splinter (Ted's nickname) failed to swing.

The Yankee pitcher walked him on four pitches. Bases loaded! Rudy York up! He already had recorded 99 runs batted in. *One more and I get a bonus from Mr. Yawkey,* I thought. *I better root.* "Come on Rudy. Show 'em what you're made of."

Rudy singled to left on the second pitch - a slow curve ball. The Sox were now ahead by a run and I had earned my bonus. *Thanks Rudy!*

In the last of the eighth inning, the Sox leading eight to three, Manager Cronin motioned to the rookie. Hey, that was me! "Grab a bat, Rook. I'm using you to pinch hit for Partee."

I was seated beside Rudy and felt a rush from my head to my toe. *Fear? Anxiety?* "I'm nervous as hell," I whispered to Rudy.

"So was I the first time I got up. Just pretend it's the Park League." Rudy glanced out to the mound at the Yankee relief pitcher. "Red Ruffing is pitching for them. He's been around too long, and he's probably not as good as some of the guys in your league."

I walked unsteadily to the bat rack, found a Rudy York model and took a few short swings, and then sat down beside the big Indian. "Mind if I use one of your bats? I don't have any Johnny Dark models yet."

Rudy grinned! "I don't know if that one has any hits left in it, but go ahead. It's only a piece of hickory, and I got more."

"What did you do the first time up in the Big Leagues, Rudy?" I anxiously asked, seeking encouragement.

"Want me to lie?"

"No! Tell me the truth."

"I was so damn nervous; I froze, watched three go by and sat down."

"Damnit Rudy - that's no help. You shoulda lied."

Rudy put a reassuring arm around my shivering shoulder. "You'll do okay, kid. Ruffing is throwing like it's batting practice. Just think about something nice. Always think about something nice when you're up there."

"What do you think about?"

"A frosty draft beer."

"Thanks Rudy! Maybe I'll think about Penny Mitchell's eyelashes." I grabbed the bat and headed for the end of the dugout. Partee was batting in the eighth slot and would be fourth up in the inning. Someone would have to get on base for me to bat. The first batter was Doerr. He struck out. The next hitter was Wally Moses. He hit a long fly ball to right - but it was caught. Two outs. I walked out into the on-deck circle as Pinky Higgins took his stance in the right-hander's batters box. Somewhere in the depths of my brain the competitive-force was battling my fear-force and was suggesting that I root for Higgins to make the third out. Then I wouldn't have to bat. Then again, my competitive force?

Higgins glanced over at me, winked and yelled so everyone could hear, "I'll save you your licks, kid. This pitcher's a washed-up bum."

Ruffing frowned and then proceeded to drill Higgins in the ribs with a fastball. Pinky grunted and started to head for the mound. Ruffing yelled something uncomplimentary as the umpire and catcher grabbed Higgins, who relented and jogged to first base, looked back and winked at me - a now very panicky rookie.

I took several deep breaths and strode to the plate. *I wonder if he deliberately taunted Ruffing so he'd hit him?* I nervously mulled over in my mind. *Maybe Pinky ain't such a prick after all.*

I took a quick sideways glance up toward Mr. Yawkey's box. *I hope Penny is watching. Or do I? What if I strike out? Rudy said to think of something nice. I'll think about keeping my elbow up and hitting the left field wall. That's what Ted recommended!*

I heard Rudy's voice from the dugout. "You can do it, Rook."

I recognized Pellagrini's voice. "I hit a homer my first at bat. Tie my record, Johnny. You can do it!"

The park announcer's voice boomed onto the field. "Attention please - batting for Partee, Jonathan Dark. That's Dark for Partee."

The sound of my name being announced sent a chill through my body. *Fuck me!* My knees felt like rubber. Rudy had said to pretend it was the Park League, and I had no trouble hitting there. Higgins had said that Ruffing was a washed-up bum. He certainly wasn't Bob Feller.

I dug into the batter's box with my spikes, waggled the bat a few times, and looked out at the large green left field wall. *I hit it several times in batting practice earlier. Why not now?*

"Batter up," the umpire called.

"Good luck, kid," the catcher whispered. "I'll tell you what Ruffing is gonna throw. You do the rest."

I turned around and sent an incredulous look at the catcher, a young kid named Berra who smiled and winked. "It's gonna be a curve," he mumbled through his metal mask.

I shrugged, turned back and resumed my stance. Ruffing wound up, checked Higgins at first, and then fired. It was a big, slow curve that I was mesmerized by. I stood there frozen as the umpire called, "Strike one!"

Rudy's voice bellowed from the dugout. "You can do it, kid. You can do it. Ruffing is throwing batting practice." Some of the fans began chanting, "Come on Dark. Hit it outta the park, Dark. Outta the park, Dark! Park it, Dark! Park it, Dark! Park it, Dark!"

Berra muttered through his mask. "Relax Rook, he's gonna throw the same pitch."

Ruffing checked on Higgins, wound up and threw the identical curve - a little slower this time. I was ready for it and swung, but too soon, and almost fell on my embarrassed face. The sweat began soaking my wool uniform, especially my arm pits. I took a deep breath. *BO! I stink!*

"You're a bum," I heard a familiar voice from the stands. *It's Nash. I can't let that scumbag see me fail. No way!*

"You stink, "Nash yelled.

Rudy yelled more encouragement. "You can do it, kid. I know you can do it. That bat's already had three hits today. There's one more in it."

Then I heard another familiar positive sounding voice from the dugout. "It only takes one pitch, and remember your elbow. You dropped it on the last swing." It was Ted Williams. *A .406 hitter is giving me advice. Hot damn!*

I felt all my muscles tighten, and then loosen. *I'm ready,* I told myself.

"He's gonna try put you away with a fastball below your knees," Berra said. "Get ready and let her rip."

The umpire chuckled. "You wouldn't tell Williams or DiMaggio what pitches were coming," he whispered to the catcher.

Berra turned his head. "This rookie ain't Ted Williams or Joltin' Joe. Besides, I remember the first time I came to the plate. Actually it was last week. The catcher told me exactly what to look for. Hell, I wet my pants - then I struck out anyway."

"You eat it, Dork," Nash's voice filtered out of the noisy stands.

"Park it Dark!" some of the more polite fans yelled.

I dug in again. Ruffing looked over at Higgins who had a short lead off first base. The pitcher wound up and fired - this time right down the middle, probably ninety miles an hour. I kept my elbow up like Ted Williams had advised and swung as hard as I could.

CRACK!

I connected!

I stood there, frozen, as I watched the ball sail out towards left field. Charlie 'King Kong' Keller, the Yankee left fielder drifted back as though he was going to catch it, and then turned and watched as the ball crashed off the Green Monster score board.

I heard Cronin's voice. "Run kid! Start running."

And I did - as fast as I could without my gimpy knee falling off. As I rounded first base the coach yelled, "Take two! Run to second."

I suddenly felt my knee give way as I went down a few feet from the bag. I embarrassedly crawled back to first base and watched as Higgins rounded third and dig for the plate. The long throw from Keller arrived just a few steps ahead of Higgins who barreled into Berra making him drop the ball. Higgins had scored the ninth Red Sox run of the day. It was driven in by rookie, Johnny Dark who sat on the first base bag - out of breath and unable to walk.

The Red Sox trainer, Johnny Orlanda bolted out of the dugout along with several of the players.

"I'm okay," I said. "I just can't walk."

Cronin waved into the dugout for a pinch runner and he then helped me to my feet and off the field with the help of Rudy York, Pellagrini, and few other players. The fans all stood and applauded. I looked back over the field. Joe DiMaggio had dropped his glove and was also clapping.

The Brownies catcher, Berra walked over to the Sox dugout and flipped me the baseball. "Save this, kid. You only get your first hit once. It took me three games to get mine."

CHAPTER FIFTEEN

BOSTON POST HEADLINES 1946

BRITAIN GRANTS INDIA INDEPENDENCE

DICK BUTTON WINS U.S. MEN'S FIGURE SKATING TITLE

MURPHY GAVE WAYNE MITCHELL'S BIO TO ME. It had been compiled by our Park League team, but it was sketchy. The important hit-man info wasn't available or known by the team owners, players, or the cops. I knew and mentally added it. The bio read: **Wayne Mitchell was born 1900 to a wealthy family in Boston's exclusive Chestnut Hill area. He attended the best private schools, was a member of the snootiest clubs, and excelled in all sports. A big boy, he worked on his physique at a local gym, eventually under an assumed name and behind his family's back. He even won some amateur heavyweight boxing bouts. At age seventeen, and upon graduation from elite Deerfield Academy and an acceptance letter from Harvard, he ran off to join the United States Army. After serving two years in the Infantry he returned home. He had learned several different ways to kill an enemy and a few tricks without a weapon. He attended Harvard, starred on the football team, graduated and went to law school, graduated and passed the bar at first try. One of his father's closest friends was the local DA, Peter Stamos. He hired Matt to work in his office. But something happened that changed the boy's life. A hit-and-run driver killed his mother. The man was apprehended, and then tried and convicted. It was the man's fourth alcohol offense. In an appeal, well-paid defense lawyers unearthed some legal formalities that ended up leading to the dismissal of the entire case. The guilty perpetrator went free. A week later the hit-and-run driver was found on the exclusive Country Club of a Brookline golf course, buried in a sand trap, only his feet exposed. His Adam's apple had been squashed. Both the victim and Wayne Mitchell were members. Suspects? There weren't any!

Over the past few years Wayne had become a pal of mine. After the weekend Park League baseball games we had shared lots of beers together, and one night the hit man filled himself with too many Crown Royals on the Rocks and then filled me in on the holes of his life's story. This is what he shared:

"DA Stamos became Judge Stamos. And then one day he called me into his office for a private meeting. I remember him telling me that he liked my style and that I reminded him of himself when he was a young whippersnapper. He had ridden with Teddy Roosevelt's Rough Riders. Hey, I knew the guy pretty well since I worked for him and as a youngster caddied for him at the Brookline Country Club. So that day one he said he might be able to use me in his new venture, and the pay was – well, it knocked my socks off. He then asked me if he could call me son. I nodded and told him that he acted more like a dad to me than my own father who never had the foggiest idea of what made me tick - or even cared. The judge then locked the door and told me that he suspected me of eliminating my mother's killer. That deduction on his part immediately scared he shit out of me. I figured that I was going to spend the rest of my life in jail. I tried to lie and told him that I didn't kill anyone. He then kiddingly accused my nose of growing. Then he fooled me and said he had no intentions of investigating the killing, and that he approved of what I did, and that he would have done the same. I had told him that I had learned in the infantry how to kill several different ways, and one of those ways was what killed the guy in the sand trap. He called what I had learned from the government a useful trade if used correctly. He then went on to explain just how many guilty parties went free because of twists and turns in the courtroom. We have the greatest legal system in the world, and it's still compromised, he said. Nothing's perfect! Nothing's ever perfect! But the guilty have got to be punished one way or another. He confessed to being a religious man and believed in God, but refused to wait around for Him to take vengeance. Too many innocent lives at stake! So the judge intended to see justice done - if I was willing to help him. From that day forward I became a hit man - a high-class hit man who only hit those who were guilty of some heinous crime. The judge would place a note explaining the pros and cons of the case along with five hundred dollars in a safe deposit box that only he and I had access to. If I didn't agree the assignment warranted the death penalty, I could rip the slip and replace it back in the box along with the cash. If I accepted the job, I took the five hundred and carried out the hit. This arrangement has been going on for over ten years."

That was the story Wayne shared with me, and I never repeated it to anyone – until now.

Penny, Wayne, Uncle Bill and I rode together down Rte. 3 to Rhode Island and Narragansett Park. It was a sunny late August day emitting a sundry of smells - exhaust fumes, country flowers, full-blossomed trees, and heavy humidity. Soon the scent of horse manure would tickle our nostrils - always a thrill to the gamblers - especially the two-dollar ones who dreamed of making that one killing that would pay up all their back bills that kept piling up week after week.

Wayne Mitchell, who Penny thought resembled John Wayne, owned a shiny 1940 Chevy convertible. Carmakers had stopped making automobiles between 1941 and 1945, so you could deem Wayne's car like new.

Penny sat between Wayne and me, crammed in the front seat, she feeling like the soft filling of a sandwich.

Uncle Bill sat in the back seat sucking oranges with one hand and handicapping with a fountain pen in the other. He frequented a local newsstand that carried the Morning Racing Telegraph - the Wall Street Journal of horseracing.

"Johnny's told me a lot about you, Wayne," Penny said, just to make conversation.

Wayne stiffened!

Penny felt it. "I - I didn't mean anything deep. I mean he told me what a good athlete you are and that you're the oldest player on the Park League team. You are the oldest, aren't you?"

"Yeah!" he answered without taking his eyes off the road. "Forty-six my next birthday. But I stay in shape. I do three hundred sit-ups every morning. Gets my blood flowing. Keeps me young and solid. I know that Johnny does one sit up and then gets out of bed." He chuckled at his own humor. "Feel my stomach."

"She hesitantly reached over and felt. "My, my, it's like steal."

"Used to be a prize fighter. In my profession a man has to stay in shape."

"And what's that," she asked.

"I saw a few of your fights at the Boston Garden," Uncle Bill interrupted. "You could'a been a contender if you'd stuck with it."

"I didn't like getting hit in the nose," Wayne said. "You ever get hit in the nose, Bill?"

Uncle Bill pointed to his leg area. "Got hit here once in 1917 - never in the nose. But once was enough, so I know what you're talking about."

"And what are you going to do for us, Mr. Mitchell?" Penny asked.

"Two things! Johnny tells me that you know about a sure thing running today. I never bet - don't believe in gambling, but I love to see them hit the top of the stretch and race for the wire. Then Johnny told me that someone threw a grenade into your apartment. I don't think that's very nice. Quite unacceptable in my circles! I'm going to see that that never happens again."

I turned up the radio hoping that Penny would stop the grilling of my friend. A silly soap opera entertained us for the next fifteen minutes.

Helen Trent! Can a woman of 35 still find happiness? Blah, blah, blah.

Wayne pulled up in front of VALET PARKING, tipped a kid a quarter and waved for Penny, Uncle Bill, and me to follow him to the dining area.

I handed Uncle Bill a pair of crutches. He could maneuver with them when absolutely necessary, and it was obligatory at the racetrack. The restaurant was on the second floor, and the facility had no elevator.

We found our RESERVED table directly beside one already occupied by Donald Nash and two very ugly, tough appearing men - probably Catalano and Rizzo. Penny's brother was nowhere in sight.

Everyone was introduced, exchanged handshakes and pleasantries, and then got down to the business of gambling.

"So what do you do for a living, Mr. Mitchell?" Nash politely asked.

"Disposal business! You know, get rid of garbage, trash - things like that."

Nash stiffened. "So you're not a cop?"

"Have no fear, Nash. I used to work in the DA's office, but never had any jurisdiction in Rhode Island."

Nash exhaled. "I got nothing to hide. I sell bonds."

Wayne moved to Nash's table and sat real close to the bogus bond salesman. "I'd like to talk to you in private, if you don't mind. Maybe you can ask your henchmen to take a walk for awhile."

Nash laughed in Wayne's face, actually spewing some spittle. "Are you kidding? My boys stay with me."

Wayne calmly took a napkin off the table and wiped his face, but his next move carried a hint of menace. He reached across the table and grabbed Catalano's shirt collar, twisted it until the man's face turned blue. "Would you please leave us alone for a few minutes? Pretty please?"

Catalano tried to push Wayne's hand away to no avail. Wayne just twisted tighter and tighter. Finally Catalano coughed and put his hands up in a surrender motion. Wayne then turned his attention to Rizzo. "How about it, Mac. I want to talk in private to your boss. I'll try my best not to hurt him."

Rizzo took a hasty look at Nash, who nodded. The two men quickly got up and left the table.

"Sorry about that scene," Wayne addressed the rest of the group. "It won't take long to straighten this low-life out."

Wayne pulled his chair closer to Nash. "Okay, bond salesman, let's start by leveling. You don't sell bonds. Right?"

Nash peeked over Wayne's wide shoulders at Penny. "I - I don't know what this's all about, but I don't have to answer any of your questions without a lawyer."

Wayne cracked a toothy smile. "You don't have to do anything, Mr. Nash. But I have a feeling that your presence around Miss Mitchell is a danger to her. Besides, I am a lawyer, and so I'm going to very nicely ask you to stay away from her until we find this grenade thrower. I'm convinced the grenade was meant for you and that attack put her life in danger. Okay?"

Nash crinkled his eyebrows and shook his head. "No one tells me what to do. Penny is my fiancée, and I tell her what's best."

Wayne shook his head. "I made a few phone calls, Nashy. I found out that you're a deadbeat bookie - one who doesn't always ante up when he loses. That could be dangerous to your health, you know. Stick the wrong gambler, and who knows what might happen. Maybe a grenade through a window?"

Nash puffed out his chest. "I'm not afraid of you."

Wayne chuckled. "You don't have to be. Are you aware that if Mr. Yawkey finds out that Penny is engaged to a bookie, he'll be forced to fire her?"

Nash scowled. "Who gives a shit? I can take care of her. She doesn't need that job."

I interrupted. "But she likes her job."

Nash flashed his middle finger. "Fuck you, Dork. No one asked you. I know you're trying to take her away from me."

Penny moved forward in her chair, spoke up, sounding perturbed. "No he isn't. He's been a complete gentlemen with me."

Catalano and Rizzo appeared on the scene. "Need any help, boss?" Catalano asked beginning to sit down, his already bulky chest puffed out.

Nash lifted his eyebrows at Wayne who shook his head. "Guess not now," Nash said. "Stay around though. I think that horse we came to watch is in the next race."

Catalano glared at Wayne and walked away.

"Want to tell me about that grenade?" Wayne asked. "Maybe I can help you stay alive."

Nash removed a Camel from a gold cigarette case, fired it up and puffed. "I don't need help from anyone. I can take care of myself."

Wayne moved his face close to Nash's - noses almost touching. "I told you that I passed the bar. Lawyers don't ever ask questions if they don't already know the answer. Now, let me say it again. Want to tell me about the grenade, who threw it, and what you plan to do about it?"

Nash flashed a frightened look for the first time. Wayne had grabbed Nash's knee under the table and was pinching the cap with strong thumb and forefinger. It felt to Nash that it was about to break off

"Okay! Okay! I - I work for a big bookmaker. Get a commission on all my deals. Once in awhile a bet comes along that I book myself. You know, something that I feel is a bad bet. I never tell my boss, and he never catches me. Two weeks ago one of my regulars gives me ten grand to put on a horse's nose. Well, on this particular bet, I know the vet who treats the horse and he tells me the nag has a bum knee. He's been giving him some undetectable drug that will eventually kill him. The vet tells me that he advised the trainer not to run the horse just yet. The owner insisted. Said to load the horse up with the drug."

"So you figured the horse would lose and you couldn't pass on an opportunity to make a killing?" Wayne suggested, sitting back in his chair, sipping his coffee. He released his vice-grip on Nash's knee.

"Yeah," Nash grunted. "Too easy, I thought. So I booked the whole thing myself, never telling my boss about it." He paused. "You can probably guess what happened. The horse forgot to die. The nag won and paid ten bucks. I owed the gambler fifty thousand. He had no sense of humor when I told him what happened. Said he'd tell my boss - and you know what that would've meant."

"So you didn't have the fifty," Wayne said, revealing a sly grin.

"Not even close. I asked for some more time, but the gambler was adamant. Gave me a week - or else!"

"So you didn't come up with the cake and he squealed to your boss, hoping he would be kind and help you?"

"Right!"

"And your boss gave you a week?"

"Right! My boss paid the debt and then gave me a week, adding ten grand onto the total. I think I was lucky to get that." Nash twitched his cheek. "Sounds like you know about these people."

"Dealt with them from the DA's office. Watched Judge Stamos put a lot of them away."

Nash hunched his shoulders and stared at Penny with somber eyes. "Sorry, Penny. I never thought they'd involve you. I love you." He reached across the table as she pulled her hands away. "I guess Mr. Mitchell is probably right. The bookies probably know where you live and threw that grenade just to scare. Didn't Dark say it was a dud?"

"Not necessarily," she said with a disgusted frown wrinkling her pretty face. "They said that the toilet water might of kept if from going off. And if Johnny hadn't acted so fast and thrown the grenade into the potty, well?"

Wayne knew he had Nash's number. "And you know that your bookie friend won't stop until the job's done?"

"Yeah, I know! And that's why I'm here today - to cash in big. Hopefully enough to pay the entire debt."

Uncle Bill and I shook our heads in unison. "And what if this horse breaks his leg, or the jockey falls off, or he just gets beat?" I piped up. "I've seen all those things happen on sure things. Haven't you?"

Nash tilted his head, not acting so tough or confident. "Yeah, I have."

"Let me tell you something, Nash." Wayne moved his chair close enough for his target to smell his aftershave. "There's a hit out on you, and you're life isn't worth a plug nickel - and you know it. Obviously you crossed the wrong people – people who use people like you as an example to others. So even if you pay, you're a dead man."

Nash began to shiver.

Wayne continued. "But, because I like Johnny here, and apparently this nice young lady had some misadvised feelings for you, I'm going to give you an out. All you have to do is leave town. Forever!" Wayne jammed a business card into Nash's sweating hand.

Nash read: "Doctor Coleman Thresher. Key West, Florida. Painless Plastic Surgery done with a smile." He looked up. "Who the hell is this guy and what does he do?"

"He does what is says on the card. I'll set up the appointment." He scanned Nash's handsome features and began touching the man's face. "Yeah, he'll like working on you. He's a masochist. Likes to make pretty people ugly." Wayne twigged Nash's nose. "He'll mash in your nose like mine. You'll look like an ex-boxer. Uh, huh. Then he'll take your sexy heavy eyelids and widen them. And your jowls? He'll fatten them. It'll cost you. But it'll keep you incognito and alive for awhile."

Nash pushed his chair out of Wayne's reach. "How do you know so much about this stuff?"

"Look, you fucking two-bit race track tout, I'm giving you a chance to live. All you have to do is take a powder today. And get the hell away from Penny. You knew they were after you and you left her in harm's way. No real man would ever do a thing like that. Even after the grenade incident you didn't own up to the fact it was meant for you. She was frightened out of her wits." Wayne stood, looming tall over the terrified man's shriveling form. "You're a creep and know it. I ought to let them kill you, but I don't want my pals getting caught up in the crossfire." He grabbed Nash's shirt collar and lightly twisted. "So you got two choices. Stick around and let them kill you. That's one. The other is to leave town in your car today. They'll be checking the trains and busses. What do you say, Nashy?"

Nash coughed as Wayne squeezed. "What do I do with my boys?"

"You tell them nothing. You don't tell anybody anything. Your only chance is to bury yourself in Key West. Most people there are fugitives, anyway. You can fish, drink, and do odd jobs. Stay there at least a year under an assumed name. Dr. Thresher also makes up false IDs. It'll cost you, so bring a few of the dollars you saved from the ten thousand dollar bet that you never made."

Nash seemed to collapse into a humble ball - all his arrogance dissolved. Even his eyes began to water. "I'm sorry,

Penny. I never wanted to hurt you. And I knew if I had told you I was a bookie, you'd never have dated me. I love you Penny. So I had to lie. Can you ever forgive me?"

Tears began to bubble up on Penny's eyes. "I can understand, Donald. I'm sorry things didn't work out."

Nash pushed Wayne's hand away from his neck and looked up at the tote board. "The fix is in on the next race. I'll give you guys the horse's name."

I reached into my wallet and pulled out two fifty-dollar bills. "I've been saving these for just this kind of horse tip." I glanced at Uncle Bill who was enjoying the excitement of Wayne roughing up Nash, and at the same time studying his racing form and making small bets. He had hit the Daily Double for a hundred and twenty-five dollars. He said to Nash, "The last tip I got broke his leg in the stretch. He was leading by eleven lengths. What's the name of your sure-thing nag? I got a hundred and twenty-five bucks burning a hole in my pocket."

"Port Henry! He's in for fifteen hundred claiming. Ran last week in the same type of race and lost by 12 lengths. The owner's been pulling him for four months. He's probably at least a ten thousand dollar horse. And it's really not fixed. It's just that Port Henry is going to try for a change. Doesn't mean the other horses don't have a chance. Port Henry is just that much better."

"So you must have talked to the jockey this morning?" Wayne suggested.

"I did! He told us last week that he thought this might be the time. That's why we're here. I make a bet for the rider. The owners also bet for the kid. If the horse wins, the jockey can't lose."

We all went to the tote windows and made our bets, except Wayne. He ordered an extra round of drinks for the group and sat back to enjoy a two-minute thrill - the most exciting two minutes in sports. Some deem it THE SPORT OF KINGS.

"Aren't you going to bet, tough guy?" Nash asked Wayne when he returned to the table.

"Never gamble," Wayne said. "But when I do something, I'm always positive it will work out."

Nash pulled his chair beside Penny and said something in her ear. She smiled politely, but shook her head and moved closer to me.

"They're in the gate," the announcer called over the loud speaker.

"I bet ten dollars to win," Penny whispered into my ear.

"For your ex-fiancée's sake," I whispered back. "I hope the horse wins so he can get away to Key West with a good nest-egg. Far away!"

Penny pulled on my sleeve and whispered again. "Do you really think Donald will leave town?"

"In my experience, when Wayne makes a suggestion to someone, they take it."

"They're off!" the track announcer called as the horses broke out of the gate. Port Henry started sluggishly and the jockey rushed him up to second place as they hit the middle of the backstretch.

"What's happening?" Penny excitedly asked, trying to sit up as high in her chair as possible. "I can't see which horse is which. They all look alike to me."

"Spring House is on top by two lengths," the announcer called. "Then Port Henry, Sunday Monster, Timely Rider, On The Money - while Writing Tips and Two Bits trail the field."

Nash started pounding his folded program on the table. "Come on, Henry. Come on Henry. My life depends on you."

Wayne poked Nash on the arm. "You didn't do what I think you did? Tell me you didn't put your whole ten grand on Henry's nose."

Nash reluctantly nodded. "What do you think?"

"Come on Henry," Wayne took up the chant, halfheartedly.

Port Henry started moving in on the leader at the top of the stretch. *One furlong to go,* I thought to myself. *1/8th of a mile.*

Henry caught a tiring Spring House in the middle of the stretch as the jockey got into his mount more vigorously with his whip. It looked like a sure win, but ---? A horse race is a horse race for a reason. It's never over until they cross the finish line. Port Henry looked like he had it won as the jockey let up on his urging. Coming on the far outside, out of view of the jockey, was a flying Two Bits.

"And here comes Two Bits," the announcer called. "It's going to be a two horse race."

Two Bits drew even with Henry about fifty yards from the wire. Their heads bobbed up and down, neither horse giving away. Henry's jockey whipped, urged, whipped and pushed. He knew what the loss would cost him. It appeared as though the two thoroughbreds hit the wire together. A dead-heat. Or maybe Two Bits won.

"Hold all tickets," the announcer's voice blared. "It's a photo finish."

"Did he win? Did he win?" Penny asked, a blank look on her face.

"The officials have to study a picture taken at the finish line," I said. "Too close to call!"

Nash's furrowed brow was wet with perspiration. "Whadaya think, guys? Did Port Henry get it?"

Wayne folded and unfolded his fingers. "He certainly didn't run like a ten thousand dollar horse. But I think he won."

The lights flashed on the infield tote board. OFFICIAL. WINNER NUMBER 2 - PORT HENRY $16.00 to win/ $8.00 to place/ $5.00 to show.

Nash clapped his hands like a little boy. "Eighty grand. I got eighty grand back from my bet. Hot damn!" He looked at Penny. "Want to come to Key West with me, baby? Eighty grand will last a long time down there."

Penny forced a small smile. "Thanks for the invite. I might have said yes several weeks ago when I thought you were a bond salesman."

Wayne pushed his chair beside Nash and put his mouth to the bookie's ear. "If I were in your shoes, I'd forget about packing a bag. Start your trip from here. You're already an hour closer to Florida. And I'd also make sure you pay your fifty grand debt. If you do your boss won't look so hard to find you."

Nash shrugged, removed a bunch of tote tickets from his wallet. "Eighty fuckin' thousand! I'm rich!" He surveyed the table's inhabitants. "Thanks gang, it's been rare. Maybe we'll run into each other some place on the road of life." He patted Wayne on the shoulder. "Thanks for your help, pal. I don't know how I'll ever repay you."

"By getting the hell out of town," Wayne uttered. "Now!"

Nash walked away, not looking back.

"Do you really think he'll take your advice," Penny asked. "He is a stubborn sort of cuss."

"He knows exactly the business practices of the goons he's dealing with," Wayne said. "And he knows that the grenade was designed to scare or kill him - not you."

Wayne turned his attention to me. "Now let's get down to the brass tacks of protecting this delicate doll. She's not safe as long as Nash's boss thinks the crooked bookie is still alive. And I doubt that Nash will share any of his winnings with his boss."

Penny stiffened. "I thought you said we'd be safe if Donald went to Florida and hid?"

"I said he'd be safe - not you or your brother."

Penny wide-eyed me with a pleading glance. "And what are you going to do about that, Mr. Bodyguard?"

"Butch might have to fend for himself. But you? You might have to stay in the houseboat for awhile." I locked eyes with Uncle Bill who nodded and cracked a smile. He was adding up his winnings. "I bet a hundred and twenty-five dollars to win, and the horse paid sixteen dollars. My math is stinky," he admitted. "Anyone want to help me add this up? There's a fresh orange in it for them."

Penny hesitated answering, realizing for the first time in a week that she was in the company of people she knew very little about. "Everything's happened so fast," she said. "The grenade, and then having to identify Majors' body – all in a few days. My life has turned upside down. I feel like I've aged at least ten years."

She removed a compact from her purse, opened it and peered into the small, round mirror. She blinked a few times, took out a powder puff and brushed her nose, nodded her head and replaced the compact in her purse. "I guess I'll have to move out of my apartment."

"Why is it that dolls always excuse themselves to powder their nose?" Uncle Bill asked, still scribbling with his pen trying to figure out his winnings before going to the window to collect. "Guys excuse themselves to take a leak," he said. "Gals say they have to powder their nose. If that's where their nose is, they got big trouble."

Wayne and I burst into a healthy laughter. Uncle Bill came up with some good jokes – mostly memorized from his afternoons at the Old Howard burlesque house.

"We do powder our noses," Penny naively insisted.

"He's only kidding," I said and touched Penny lightly on the shoulder. "I'm afraid you're going to take a leave of absence from your job. I don't want these bums finding you and asking any questions."

Wayne nodded.

"The horses are coming onto the track for the fourth race," the announcer called. "Make your bets early. Don't be shut out."

"Like anybody ever gets shut out," Wayne murmured. "Let's get out of here." He turned his attention to Penny. "You've got to tell your brother about what went down here today, and tell him to lay low. Do you think he'll do it?"

"I don't know. He's awfully independent, and he does think he knows everything. Ever meet anybody who was born knowing all the answers? That's my brother. Hard to teach anybody anything if they already know."

"Met a few," Wayne nodded. "It's toughest if they're someone you like. But if you want, I'll talk to him."

She looked anxiously at me. "Maybe Johnny can talk to him. Uh, huh! I think I'd rather Johnny talk to him. Do you mind?"

CHAPTER SIXTEEN

BOSTON POST HEADLINES 1946

PHILIPPINES GAIN INDEPENDENCE FROM U.S.

U.S.A. DROPS A-BOMB ON BIKINI ATOLL, 4TH ATOMIC EXPLOSION

IN HIS LATE SIXTIES, skinny, a black fedora covering maybe a bald head, and a corncob pipe hanging out of the side of his mouth like Popeye, Uncle Bill Dark fancied himself a gourmet cook and loved to dabble in fish recipes. As a matter of fact, he actually resembled Popeye.

My office desk and three small file cabinets took up one wall of the houseboat living room. A console radio sat in another corner. A wood burning pot bellied stove in the middle of the room played home to a large steaming pot. Uncle Bill had purchased a few fresh lobsters from the next barge - The J.C. Hook Company.

"Smells like lobster," Penny said as she followed Uncle Bill and me into the houseboat's innards. "What's the blackboard for? I didn't notice that before."

One entire wall was covered with a huge blackboard like those used in local schools.

"It's how Johnny figures his cases," Uncle Bill answered. "After supper we'll give him a hand. Detective Murphy's dropping by with clues on the Majors' killing. He thinks it was an amateur job made to look professional."

Penny sank deep into a cushioned easy chair, a sad look on her face. "Maybe Mr. Yawkey was on the right track after all."

"What track was that, young lady?" Uncle Bill asked.

"He hired Johnny thinking that one of the ballplayers murdered Majors."

I disappeared into the bathroom. When I reappeared I had traded my business shirt for a wooly white sweater. I fired up a Chesterfield, blew a large smoke ring, and then a smaller one through it. "Takes a lot of practice to do great tricks like that," I said with a grin.

"I'm impressed," Penny said. "Can you teach me?"

"I'm sure Johnny could teach you a lot of things, young lady," Uncle Bill added his two cents. "But if I were you, I'd not get too involved. He's a nice kid, and all. Hey, I brought him up. But you look like the marrying kind. Two kids, nice little house surrounded by a white picket fence - and, of course, a dog. That's not Johnny's style. He don't commit!"

I ignored my uncle's remarks and set three places at a fold-up card table.

"I'll help," Penny started to rise from her chair.

I stopped her. "No, no! You're our guest. We don't have many of those around here. Especially ones that glow like you."

All three of us jumped as we heard a knock on the door.

"It's only Murph," Uncle Bill said. "Come on in. The door's unlocked."

Detective Murphy entered, bowed to Penny and took a seat on a small sofa. "Didn't mean to interrupt your dinner, gang. I can come back later."

Uncle Bill wheeled himself over to the console and flipped it on. Jim Britt and Tom Hussey were announcing the Red Sox lineup for the next day's game against Yankees. They also announced that Rookie Jonathan Dark had been released. Injured knee!

"Interesting career for the Dark kid," Britt said. "One at bat and one hit. That's a batting average of one thousand."

"Hooray from me," I said with a smile. "But Cronin wants a 25th man on the team who can play. I understand! And Mr. Yawkey still wants me to solve the case and protect Penny." I removed my apron, walked over to the blackboard and proceeded to write. FRANK MAJORS. 20. DECEASED. MURDERED. BAD HABITS: DOPE. BOOZE. MAYBE GAMBLING. WOMEN. LIST OF PEOPLE WITH POSSIBLE MOTIVES: I wrote down all the players who I had been led to believe had a motive, I had talked to, and then exonerated. A LOCAL DOPE DEALER. ROY PARTEE.

I turned my attention to Murphy and said, "Majors tried to sleep with Partee's wife. Partee threatened to kill him." I proceeded to write: OTHER SUSPECTS: DONALD NASH, PENNY'S BROTHER, AND ---.

"Stop there," Murphy said. "Why are they suspects?"

I glanced at Penny and lifted my eyebrows.

She hesitated, and then nodded. I cupped my hand and whispered something into Murphy's ear.

"Oh, sorry Penny," Murph said. "I didn't mean to bring up a sore subject. Actually, I hate to say this, but that gives you the best motive. But I can't fathom you mixing cement."

Penny forced a laugh.

Uncle Bill relit his pipe. "If this punk was doing dope he could've run into anybody that might've killed him." He looked at Murphy. "You say it appeared to be professional?"

"Appeared!" he said. "But the coroner discovered a strange cut near Majors' heart, and it wasn't from a fish bite."

I wrote the new information on the blackboard, POSSIBLE KNIFE WOUND, and then asked, "And what caused the cut, Murph?"

"How about a large pair of scissors," he answered.

I erased KNIFE and replaced it with SCISSORS.

"So he might have died before he was put under the pier?" Penny asked.

"Not really!" Murph answered. "The scissors were superficial. But I've never run into a professional who carried a pair of scissors, unless he owned a barber shop."

We all laughed and then jumped when we heard a knock on the door.

"Who visits you guys at this time of night and in the rain?"

"Only one way to find out," Murphy said. "Come in. The door is open."

A tall, hunched over man wearing a long overcoat and brimmed beret entered. He coughed and raised his chubby face. He immediately looked familiar to me, but a lot older and tired than the last time I had seen him.

"Babe?" Uncle Bill exclaimed, his face lighting up. "Come on in and join us in a drink. Haven't seen you all season."

"Do you think us kids will all fit?" he joked, pulled off his overcoat and slumped down on the couch beside Murphy. His eyes were puffy, his hair thin and graying. I hadn't seen him since he'd been forced to retire from the Braves team in 1935. The fifty-two year old man had aged at least thirty years. They say that a fast burning candle only burns half as long. George Herman Ruth had always been a fast burning candle. I poured him a tall glass of scotch with a few cubes. The Babe downed it in one gulp, and then burped. He lit a smelly stogie, nodded hello to Penny and puffed. "I'm cutting back on all my bad habits," he said and laughed in a scratchy voice. "Hey, Billy boy, remember when I played for the Sox and had a room in the Red Light District?" The Babe had started his Major League career with the Red Sox in 1914 as a pitcher – a great one. They sold him to the Yankees in 1920.

Uncle Bill allowed a small smirk. "I remember! And I recall one night you had four girls crammed into your double bed. After staying up all night and making two quarts of scotch disappear, you showed up at Fenway five minutes before the game and then proceeded to smack out two homers."

It was the Babe's turn to smirk. "Sorry lady! Didn't mean to reminisce in front of you." He turned to the rest of the group. "Anybody going to introduce me to this dishy doll?"

I jumped up. "Sorry, Babe. This is Mr. Yawkey's private secretary, Penny Mitchell. She's staying with us awhile."

The Babe stood up and bowed. "Nice to meetcha, kid." He noticed the blackboard. "And what are you kids up to with all that crap on the blackboard? A murder case, I hope."

Uncle Bill had stayed in touch with the Babe all these years and had explained how his nephew used the blackboard when on a tough caper.

I refilled Ruth's now empty glass. "Are you good at keeping secrets?" I asked the Babe.

"Are you kidding, kid? Whatever you tell me today, I'll forget tomorrow. I think they call it amnesia - or something. It either comes with old age or abused bodies."

The Babe stood up, walked to the board and began studying. "I recognize some of these names. Who got murdered and why?"

I eyed Murph who eyed Bill who eyed Penny. No one seemed to object so I finally nodded and asked, "Ever heard of Stephen Majors? He struck out 27 batters in an Industrial League game last year. Mr. Yawkey signed him and the youngster attended Spring Training with the team."

The Babe scratched his graying hair. "I think so. The team left him in Florida for some reason. He got sick or something."

"He got sick alright," Bill said. "He discovered dope and Mr. Yawkey hired a private rehab doctor. Probably should have sent him to a rehab center."

"And he murdered someone?" Babe asked.

"No," Murphy answered. "He got murdered. The punk was a wisenheimer who tried to sleep with any broad who wasn't nailed down."

The Babe scanned the board again. "And these are the suspects? Hey, I used to screw around a lot and no one ever murdered me."

I spoke seriously. "I agree! I really don't think he was killed by one of the jealous players. I've talked to almost all of them – none acting in any way guilty of anything other than thinking that the kid is a dopey asshole. That's why you see that most of their names have been crossed off. By the way, you can cross out Mace Brown and Eddie Pellagrini."

The Babe picked up a piece of chalk and started scribbling. "Ever see Dick Powell in Murder My Sweet? He plays that private eye – Marlowe. I don't read all that much, but I read all of Raymond Chandler's stuff in Black Mask's monthly mystery magazine."

"I read that too," I said. "And I'm a Hammett fan. Sam Spade. I hate to admit that it's where I learned to be a private eye."

"Do you guys know that the baseball commissioner made a rule that all the vets who came home from the war could stay on the team's roster, major or minor league for two years if they'd played before either joining up or being drafted?" Babe was writing names of players.

"So what?" Bill asked.

"Well, I was quite upset when the Yankees asked me to take a hike. I probably should have killed Colonel Rupert, the owner, but I like to think I'm a little civilized. And I have to admit it crossed my mind - especially when I'm clearing my scratchy throat with this medication." He swigged the last drops of his second scotch. "I'm writing down last year's line-up. I'm still a fan and think I can remember who played. How many of these guys lost their jobs because Johnny's, Teddy's, Dom's, Bobby's came marching home?"

1945 – LAST YEAR'S STARTING LINEUP PLAYERS. EDDIE LAKE, PAUL CAMBELL, and JOHNNY LAZOR – he continued to write. "I can't recall the whole team, but you can see none of last year's regulars are still starting, and most of them have gone home or back to the minors."

He then wrote: 1946 STARTING LINE-UP: YORK at first, DOERR at second, PESKY at short, and HIGGINS at third with RIP RUSSELL. Outfield: WILLIAMS in left, DI-MAGGIO in center and MOSES and CULBERSON in right. WAGNER catching. PARTEE and McGAH are backup catchers. GUTTERAGE is a backup infielder. He looked up. "Did I leave anyone out?"

Penny smiled and looked impressed. "Holy smoke! You must be a Red Sox fan," she said. "I would think you'd be a Yankee fan. That's where you played most of your career, isn't it?"

Ruth made a face. "Are you kidding, kid? They screwed and tattooed me royally. I pleaded for the manager's job and they ditched me. Hey, without me they'd never have been the great Yankees. And you know what they call Yankee Stadium."

"The House That Ruth Built," Penny said.

The Babe smiled and bowed.

"Hey, you left out most of the pitchers," Murphy said. "Any reason for that?"

"Yeah! A good reason! Most all of last year's regular pitchers were dumped right away – even before Spring Training. One of the guys who stayed was recently dumped."

"And who was that, Sherlock?" Bill asked.

"Not Sherlock! Call me Spade or Marlowe. This is what they'd come up with." He let some thick cigar smoke circle his head. "How many players can a major league team carry on the roster?"

I quickly answered. "Twenty-five! So what?"

"So, when they activated Majors, one of the players hadda be dropped. Right?"

Us three men nodded.

"Who was it?" Babe asked, his piece of chalk poised to write the name.

Murphy shrugged, as did Bill and me.

Penny raised her hand. She knew! "Charlie Wilson! He was a starter in 1944 and 45. He wasn't very good. Won only nine games last year, and became a mop-up guy this year. He pitched when we were way ahead or way behind."

The Babe walked over to the table holding the scotch bottle and refreshed his own glass, burped and sat down on a wooden stool in front of the blackboard. "You guys got any idea what that could cost Wilson? Players get extra money for getting into the World Series, and even more if they win it. So, do you think he has a right to be upset at Majors, especially if he thinks Majors is a punk?"

I walked to the blackboard and wrote in caps, CHARLIE WILSON. "Thanks Babe. Need a job as a sidekick? You know, like Tonto to the Lone Ranger, or Dr. Watson to Sherlock Holmes?"

"Thanks for the offer, kid. But I'm too busy trying to get my golf handicap into the single digits. I try to play everyday. It's the most humbling thing I've ever undertaken. Hey, hitting a 90-mile per hour baseball was easy as pie compared to trying to hit that little dimpled-faced plastic ball that sits still right under your nose and doesn't even wiggle. I can hit it over three hundred yards."

Murphy interrupted and asked Penny, "Know where this Charlie Moore lives?"

"He was staying at the Kenmore. Mr. Yawkey paid for his room for the rest of the month, but maybe he went home. I haven't seen him since he was released."

"Did he say anything derogative when Mr. Yawkey told him?" Murphy asked.

"The manager informed him. Mr. Yawkey shies away from negative stuff."

"Let me check on Wilson's whereabouts," Murphy said and then motioned me to follow him outside.

"Wait for us," Babe said. "I'm wheeling Bill around the corner to Del's Deli for a few more drinks. We got some catching up to do."

Penny cleared off the table and started the dishes. Soft music played on the radio in the background. A young kid named Frank Sinatra was singing: I can't give you anything but love. *Hmm! I wonder!*

Murphy and I sat on the houseboat deck overlooking the harbor. "So where does that leave us now that Mr. Nash has flown the coop with your help?" he asked, perturbed. "Seems as though you know some stuff you're not revealing. And what do think about Babe's theory?"

"Nash was never a suspect, and I'm sorry I didn't tell you about the fixed race. But now I think we should be looking into Mr. Wilson. Maybe he left town and we can erase him off the blackboard, and I'm really not sure we really give a damn who killed Majors. He was a creep, a doper, and pissed everyone off. I assume your department has more important fish to fry?"

"I agree he's dirt," Murph nodded. "But I just can't brush it under the rug." He hesitated for a moment and studied my demeanor.

"Why not?" I asked. "Are you starting to think about the scissors? They're certainly more of a girly thing?" I peaked into the living room. Penny appeared to be asleep on the sofa. Uncle Bill was still out with the Babe. The radio droned softy in the corner of the room. Dick Haymes was singing about June busting out all over. A seagull sat on a piling just outside the living room window appearing to spy on the activities of the houseboat. I went inside and pulled the long corded phone outside and handed it to Murphy who quietly dialed the Kenmore Hotel, identified himself and asked if Charles Wilson had checked out, and if he had, when?"

He waited!

His eyebrows lifted and then he hung up. "Maybe the Babe should apply for a PI license. Wilson is still around. At least he didn't check out yet."

The phone ringing startled both of us. I picked up. It was Rudy. "Sorry they let you go kid," Rudy said, sincerely. "But you did get that one off the wall. No one can ever take that away from you."

"Thanks Rudy! You're right! I'll never forget that exhilarating feeling. The players have probably already heard all about

Majors. The cops are doing Mr. Yawkey a favor and keep it out of the papers, but, well ---."

"Yeah! The cops have been questioning everyone around here. I understand that Mr. Yawkey is headed back this way from his vacation." An extended pause became uncomfortable.

"Rudy! Rudy! You still there?"

"Yeah, kid! Hey, I gotta tell you something. That's really why I called. Maybe something I shoulda told you before. But I didn't tell the cops."

"Yeah Rudy, I'm all ears."

"That last night that Majors was around he was high as a kite. He left me and said he was going to Penny's apartment. He told me that she loved him. Well, I got thinking about what a bullshitter he was, but it wasn't any of my business. Well, he came home the next morning. It looked like he'd slept in his clothes. He napped 'till noon, and then we had lunch and went to the ballpark together. It was an afternoon game with Detroit. I hit a homer and so did Ted."

"Yeah, so what? What happened?"

"That next night he said he was going back to her apartment. You know, the last time anyone saw him. We all knew that she was engaged to Nash and didn't like Majors." York paused. "And again, he was high as a kite. Ya know?"

I knew! "So what happened?"

"I phoned her."

"And?"

"She picked up! I apologized for it being so late, and then told her about what Majors had said and warned her that he was all doped up again. She thanked me and said he wasn't there and she didn't expect him. Well, you know the rest. Or, I guess no one knows the rest. He was never seen again after that night."

I pondered the new information, came to no conclusions, and thanked my former roommate and congratulated him on the Red Sox win. "Wait a sec, Rudy. Have you seen Charlie Wilson lately?"

Rudy didn't answer.

"Rudy! Charlie Wilson, the pitcher who was released when Majors came on board."

"He's a fairy," Rudy whispered.

"That's not the point, Rudy. I have reason to believe he's still in town. He may have got mad at Major's for taking his job and decided to kill him. At least he had a motive."

"I don't think so."

"You don't think he's still around or you don't think he killed Majors?"

"I don't think he killed Majors. But I know where he is right now if you want to question him."

"Yeah, Okay," I said. "I want to know."

"Ever hear of the Hermaphrodite House?"

"Isn't it a bar?"

"It's a joint where three-dollar bills hang out. Do you know what a Hermaphrodite is?"

"Is it someone born with both sexual organs?" I thought I knew and asked.

"I think so. That's where Charlie hangs out."

"Do they stay open this late?"

"How the hell do I know? I'm no fruitcake. Call 'em. They're in Scollay Square."

"Thanks for the info, roomy," I said and hung up.

"Who was that?" Murphy asked.

"Rudy York."

"And?"

"Rudy told me that Wilson hangs out at a queer joint in Scollay Square. Maybe we should check it out."

"Why the hell didn't you tell me?"

"I just did!"

"Oh, yeah. You did! Well then, let's go. Shall we act like fruits?"

"I don't know. How do fruits act?"

Murph shrugged. "Hold hands?"

I visibly cringed. "Maybe, but no kissing."

We both jumped when they heard a noise behind us. It was Penny.

"I just woke up, but overheard about Wilson and the fairy joint. If you're going out, I'm going with you. Nash took me into that bar one evening. I think someone owed him some money. He said it was to do with bonds. But I knew different. They do kiss each other and hold hands. It's kind of grundy."

"You sure you want to go with us?" I asked, hoping she'd say no.

"I sure as hell don't want to stay here alone and try and catch a flying grenade."

Us guys eyeballed each other for a few seconds, and then both nodded. "Okay! We're going slumming to Scollay Square. Maybe we'll find Murph a date - a burlesque dancer."

CHAPTER SEVENTEEN

BOSTON POST HEADLINES 1946

WEIGHT WATCHERS FORMED

SYRIA'S INDEPENDENCE FROM FRANCE RECOGNIZED

WE HAILED A CAB, gave directions to Scollay Square, probably a mile away. We sat back and discussed our approach if we found Wilson.

"Fingerprints?" I suggested and asked Murphy. "Were there fingerprints anywhere? I don't expect anyone finds fingerprints on a dead body that's been washed over in the harbor."

"Nothing we could pinpoint," Murphy said.

"How about just arrest him?" Penny suggested.

"On what grounds?" Murphy asked. "I can't just arrest someone because he's queer."

"A suspect?" I said

"Have to have reasonable cause," Murphy said. "Hey, you were a cop. You know that."

The cabby pulled up in front of a dilapidated 4-story hotel – the first floor, a bar dance joint – HERMAPHRODITE HOUSE. I gave the cabby a two-dollar bill. "Keep the change, bud," I said. "I don't have any threes on me – yet!"

I waited for someone to laugh. Nothing! *Bad joke in this part of town,* I finally deduced.

We went inside a smoke filled, low ceiling bar. The room was semi-dark and filled. The music filtered from a nickel jukebox – one that you can ask for a song and a live voice answers – and then plays. I always wondered where the voice hung out. *In the basement?* I never found out.

Wall booths surrounded the area and featured an island type bar – long and busy - three bartenders pouring as fast as the orders were given.

"Do you think everyone in here is queer?" Penny asked.

"Shh," I warned. "Someone will hear you. "We aren't queer, but everyone here probably thinks we are. I mean - I hope they do. We're supposed to be undercover and looking for Charlie Wilson. Do you see him?"

"Are you kidding?" Penny said and punched my arm. "I can hardly see you through this smoke."

"Let's mosey up to the bar," Murph suggested. "This is going to be a dandy evening. Hey, Johnny, if you're hit on, you gotta make it look good. Can you dance?"

I grimaced. "Are you kidding? I'm not dancing with you."

"I'm kidding! If someone wants to dance with you, just tell the guy you're having your period."

Penny punched Murph on his arm. Hard!

We found three empty seats at the bar and ordered. "Three drafts," Murphy said, taking the lead. "I'll chase mine with a shot of scotch."

The bartender, bow tied and pasty faced, smiled wide, tilted his head and winked a few times at Murph. "Haven't seen you fellas around heah befah." He had the quintessential Bahston accent. "You're kinda cute. Yah know that?" He was addressing Murphy - or mentally undressing him.

Murphy acted nervous. "Hell with being undercover," he said and removed his wallet, flipping it open and revealing his badge. "We're looking for someone."

"Oopsie daisy," the bartender said. "I just work heah. I don't know nobody."

"How about a Red Sox baseball player?" I asked and greased the man's palm with a crisp one-dollar bill. "He's big, dark hair, and cute. You'd know him. Charlie Wilson!"

"You want his autograph?" the bartender asked. "I can get that for you. And you can keep the money."

I waved the dollar away. "We need the man, not his signature. Seen him tonight?

The bartender fondled the bill, smiled and said, "He's in the furthest back booth. It's dahk there. Stuff happens!" He eyed Murphy. "You better stay here. I'd get fired if anyone gets in trouble because of me."

Murphy nodded. "I understand! Keep the scotches coming. My friend here will take care of Wilson."

I whispered into Penny's ear. "Come with me. I don't want to get picked up." I removed the Red Sox notebook from my back pocket hoping that Wilson's bio was in it. It was!

Charlie Wilson is a thirty-five year old pitcher who never got a chance in the Major Leagues until 1944 when he was invited to Spring Training with the Red Sox. He had won fifteen games in the Northern New England Industrial League, a semi-pro organization. He's tall, thin, soft-spoken and friendly. He has a fair fastball and good curve – good enough to win him a regular job on a depleted ball team that most of the stars had long since gone into the Armed Services. Charlie has flat feet that qualified him a 4F classification. He won nine games in 1945, and has high hopes for 1946.

Wilson was seated in a booth that was located in a far corner of the room. It was dark and smoky and had a curtain that could be pulled across the front for privacy. The curtain was open. Another man sat across from him - a football fullback size guy with muscles on muscles, ugly black, sleeveless T-shirt showing off shoulder-to-wrist tattoos. He sported a wiffle, and needed a shave – badly. *Scary!* I approached with Penny. "That's him," she said. "He looks like hell."

"Which one?"

"Not the monster!"

"Is he a drinker?"

"Not that I know of. He never drank with Mr. Yawkey's regular crew."

"Excuse me," I said, approaching the two men. "Don't mean to interrupt you. My name is Jonathan Dark. I'm a private investigator. I'm sure you recognize Mr. Yawkey's secretary, Penny Michaels?"

Wilson politely stood up and extended his hand. "Of course I know Penny. Please join us. Our pleasure!"

I noticed that Wilson appeared tired and was drinking coffee. The big man was drinking a draft.

"Thank you," I said. "I have a few questions that maybe you can help me with. I won't take much of your time."

"No problem! For the first summer in many years I have more time than I know what to do with. Maybe you know that I was let go by the Sox." He sipped his coffee, studied my face and then blurted, "Hey, aren't you the kid that got his first hit in the last ballgame? Hot damn! I think that's swell."

Penny and I pushed ourselves into the booth as the other two men moved over. A waiter noticed the new arrivals and approached us. "Can I get you two anything?" he asked with a lisp.

Penny's eyes questioned mine.

"Two coffees, please" I said.

"How can I help you, Mr. Dark?" Wilson asked. "And congratulations on that hit. It was a doozy." He poked his big friend in the overly muscled arm. "Hey Bull, this guy got a hit his first time up in the bigs. Whaddaya you think about that?"

The goon didn't answer, but his cautious eyes studied both intruders.

"By the way," Wilson said, "this is a friend of mine, Bull Brown. He's a wrestler. Gonna tangle Steve Crusher Casey at the Arena Saturday night."

Brown's face remained rigid as he reached across the table and surrounded my hand with his very large fist. "Nice to meetcha, Dark," he said. "You don't look like you belong in a place like this."

I pulled my hand away. "Neither do you."

"Don't judge da book by da jacket," he said. "No one judges me in here, and I think if my fans knew I hung around in a joint like dis, it'd be curtains for my career. So I'd appreciate it if you two would keep it under your doibies."

"Our lips are buttoned," Penny said.

"I'm looking into the disappearance of Steve Majors," I interrupted, addressing Wilson. "Can you shed any light on him?"

Wilson went silent.

"Can I tell em?" Brown asked, leaning forward and whispering.

Wilson shrugged and then nodded.

The waiter brought two coffees and refreshed Brown's draft.

"Charlie and Majors were lovers," Brown said after the waiter had left the area. "They met in Florida at Spring Training. Charlie was crushed when the Red Sox dropped him off the roster. Just before the season started he had a chance to latch onto the St. Louis Browns, but hung around here just to be with Majors. Then Majors disappeared and Charlie found out that the Browns weren't interested anymore. Tough break! Totally screwed up his baseball career."

I felt my stomach drop a few inches. I hunched my shoulders. "You're saying that Majors was a switch hitter?"

"I knew he loved the dames," Wilson said, almost apologetically. "But he and I had something special. I think I really understood him, and I think I coulda kept him on the straight and narrow."

I spent a few seconds digesting the shocking information, and then looked up and asked, "When's the last time you saw him?"

"Here! A little over a week ago," Wilson answered and looked directly at Penny. "He said he was going over to see Penny. He told me that she was after him - was in love with him. He told me that he was going to tell her to take a hike."

Penny sat forward. "He was lying," she said in a voice too loud. "I hated him. I ---."

"Hush up!" I said softly and put a strong hand on her knee. "You and I know the truth." I turned back to Wilson. "I've some bad news for you, Charlie."

"About Penny and Majors? I told you that he said he wasn't in love with her and I believed him. She's cute and all that, but ---."

"Majors is dead," I injected, matter of factly. "He was murdered."

Wilson froze and then put his hands over his face and broke into tears. The big wrestler put his arms around his friend. "Couldn't you have broken the news to him a little gentler?" Brown said, frowning. "He told ya he was in love with Majors. Don't you have any passion at all?"

Penny and I stared at each other for a long moment. Wilson kept crying, out of control, the big goon cuddling his head in his arms.

I dropped a five-dollar bill on the table and then Penny and I headed quickly for the door. "Wilson isn't our killer," I informed her out of the two other men's earshot. "We're back to square one."

CHAPTER EIGHTEEN

BOSTON POST HEADLINES 1946

JACKIE ROBINSON DEBUTS AT 2ND BASE FOR DODGER MINOR LEAGUE TEAM

BILL DICKEY REPLACES JOE MCCARTHY AS NY YANKEE MANAGER

AFTER MURPHY HAD BEEN INFORMED of the latest information, Penny and I went back to the houseboat. Penny buried herself on the couch while I bustled around, cleaning up, and jamming the smelly lobster shells into a bag and then throwing them over the side into the harbor.

Penny stirred. "What time is it, Johnny?" she asked and rubbed her eyes. She was wearing a silk skirt that had ridden up almost to her thighs revealing a swell pair of legs, black panties with garter belts hooked to sheer nylon stockings - one sporting a long run from the knee to the toe. Nylons were still hard to come by, but I figured that they must have been a gift from Nash. I felt aroused and had trouble keeping my eyes above her waist. She noticed, blushed, and straightened her skirt.

"It's past midnight," I said. "Bill's asleep. Want something to drink?"

"Water?"

"I'll join you."

I removed some ice from the icebox and poured two large tumblers of water. "Here, let's go outside on the deck and watch the moon play games with the waves. You'll find it relaxing."

Penny followed. The deck surrounded the entire barge and protruded about six feet out into the water. Two badly worn chaise lounges appeared to be the only seats.

"You take the one without the hole in the seat and the wooly blanket," I courteously invited.

Penny lay back and sipped at her water glass. "It is serene here," she said. "And it seems safe. Anyone ever bother you around the waterfront?"

"Just a few rats and drunks. I knife the rats and wave my knife at the drunks."

Penny turned sideways, fluttered her eyelashes. "Do you think I'll be safe here with you?"

My chaise was almost touching hers. I reached out and ran my fingers through her hair that was beginning to stiffen from the thick salt air. "That night that Majors tried to attack you?"

Her eyes widened. "Yes? I try not to think about it."

"That was the last time you ever saw him? Just that one night? Not the next night – the night he disappeared? The night that Wilson was referring to."

"The night before he supposedly disappeared. Yes! I never saw him after the night I told you about."

"Are you sure?"

She threw off the blanket and sat up, shivering. "I - I don't know what you're trying to say, Johnny. I wouldn't lie to you. Please don't ask any more questions. You're scaring me and I'm tired."

I delicately pulled Penny off her chaise over on top of me and began hugging. "I've been wanting to do this since the first time I saw you in Mr. Yawkey's office. Do you mind?"

She cuddled closer and moaned, "I like that shell part story. Do you think we fit?"

I nuzzled closer, my hands lightly rubbing her back. "So far," I whispered. "And I think it's worth checking."

She lifted her head and stared deeply into my eyes. Her breath was heavy - matching mine.

"Can anyone see us?" she asked and pulled away.

"Only the fish, seagulls, and rats." I maneuvered myself closer to her and placed my hands under the back of her thin sweater and began lightly rubbing her bare skin.

She moaned! "That feels good. But please cut it out with the rat stuff, will ya? Girls don't like mice, so they certainly can't feel romantic with rats around."

"Who's talking about being romantic?"

Penny shocked me by forcefully pressing her lips against mine for a long moment, and then pulled back and said, "Please stop talking and let's get this show on the road. But I have to confess something."

"What's that?"

"I'm still a virgin."

I sighed relief that she hadn't confessed to any crimes and quickly fumbled with a snap on the back of her bra, and finally unhooked it. I then slid the sweater over her head and gently pulled my face between her ample breasts.

I can't breathe, I thought. *But what a way to die.*

When we were both satiated, I lit a Chesterfield and shared it with her. "Did it hurt?" I whispered. "I tried to be as gentle as possible. I really can't control him."

On my twenty-first birthday Uncle Bill finally told me about the Birds and the Bees. Obviously, I knew a little bit about them – but pretended I didn't just to humor him. I recall that he informed me that female virgins had what's called a cherry, and when they had sex for the first time the cherry broke and bled. Penny wasn't the first time for me by a long shot, but I had never cared if my partner was a virgin, hooker, or ----? Sometimes I didn't even know her name. Penny was the first woman I had ever really cared about. And I was head over heels in love.

"Him? Who's him?" she asked in a soft, sexy whisper.

I chuckled. "You know who him is."

Penny mimicked my cackling chuckle. "It only hurt a little," she moaned, tiny tears in her eyes. "But it was worth it."

"Sorry!"

"You were gentle. Thanks!"

"Did you ever wonder why people smoke after sex," I asked as I leaned down to straighten her panties, really checking for any sign of blood. *Hey, I'm a private investigator, aren't I? I told myself. I'm just harmlessly investigating. Aren't I?*

"I give up," Penny answered, spreading her legs a bit, seeming to enjoy the attention.

"No - I'm serious. I wonder what Murph does after sex. He quit smoking."

Penny pulled the blanket up over our heads as a cool breeze flitted in off the harbor. "What if it was the other way around?" she asked.

"Like how?"

"Like a person had to have sex after every cigarette."

I laughed quietly. "I like that scenario. Uh, huh. I'd like that better, and I like your sense of humor. Are you ready?"

"For another cigarette?"

"No, silly girl. You know!"

We slept huddled together, well blanketed on the deck floor. No one kept count as to how many times we made love, but when we watched the sun rise over the city behind us, and smelled bacon cooking from Bill's stove, we decided that we liked each other and we were definitely fortunate shell parts who had found their mates.

CHAPTER NINETEEN

BOSTON POST HEADLINES 1946

BANK OF ENGLAND NATIONALIZES ANTI-BRITISH DEMONSTRATION IN EGYPT

I CHECKED INTO THE BERKLEY STREET PRECINCT after being summoned by my friend, Detective Murphy. I had showered at home, eaten a heavy breakfast prepared by Uncle Bill, and made Penny promise to stay on the houseboat until I returned. "Open the door for no one," I warned.

I hi-signed my old buddies as I entered Murphy's office.

"Sidown, pal," the big redheaded cop said. "You might not like this, but I got some bad news." He paused! "Then, on the other hand, maybe good news."

I felt a chill pass down my spine.

"We got Penny's brother in custody for the murder of Steve Majors."

I contemplated the information. *Good? Maybe!* I fired up a cigarette and inhaled deeply. "What led you to him?"

"We searched Penny's apartment and found a pair of scissors. We checked them and found just a trace of blood. Coincidentally - Major's blood. Butch dropped by just as we were leaving and said they were his scissors."

I felt anger heat the back of my neck. *Something ain't right!* "So, what made you search Penny's apartment in the first place? Without a warrant the scissors won't even be admissible in court? And they didn't kill him, anyway. You know that. Someone could have been clipping his beard, or something. He could have cut himself."

Murphy cracked a smile. "The grenade and your blackboard led us to the search. We plan to check everyone on your chalk list."

"You think maybe Butch thinks his sister killed Majors and is taking the wrap?"

Murphy nodded and continued. "I already talked to the DA. I don't think the scissors will produce anything in the way of condemning prints other than maybe whoever was in the apartment. Penny, the brother, Nash, you, and who knows who else. But it scared the kid enough so he confessed to the killing."

I did a double take. "What did he say? Why did he kill Majors?"

"He says that Majors came back the next night after he had tried to rape his sister, pushed his way into the apartment, was high and insisted on waiting for Penny. He told Butch that they were lovers."

"So Butch butchered him?'

"You could say that."

"Alone?"

"Butch said that Penny wasn't there when it happened."

"That's what her brother said? What about after it happened?"

"He said he took the body away and never told his sister what had happened."

"Someone isn't telling the whole truth and nothing but the truth," I said and rubbed my recently shaved chin.

"What's wrong with the confession?" Murphy asked.

"Penny says that Majors never came over to her house that last night. But Butch says he did. So someone's lying."

"I'm just telling you what the kid told me."

"Self defense? An accident?" I questioned.

"We haven't got to that part yet. We felt he should consult a lawyer, so we got him one. He's with him now. I don't know what they'll claim or admit."

"Did he tell you that he put Major's feet in cement?" I asked. "He couldn't have gotten that from the newspaper because it wasn't in the newspaper. They haven't even printed an obituary yet."

"Yup! He said he did. But his sister could have told him about that fact. Don't forget, she identified the body."

"So where did he say he got that brilliant idea of the professional hit?"

"A James Cagney movie!"

"I gotta go back to the houseboat," I said, feeling baffled. "Uncle Bill is guarding Penny until I get there. Then I'd like to question Butch. Will that be okay with you?"

Murphy flashed an I-don't-give-a-shit-look. "Anything I can help you with, pal? By the way, are you withholding anything that I should be apprised of?"

"I got one thing that's been puzzling me," I said. "I questioned quite a few of the players about Majors. They all hated him. A few even had motives to kill him. Several of them served in the Navy or Army, and I'm sure they learned how to kill people – and maybe some of them did – legally in the line of duty, of course."

Murphy furrowed his brow. "That's one of the downsides of war. You know that!"

I nodded! "Well, this one guy, Eddie Pellagrini, a utility infielder suggested that maybe Majors' drug habit was being fed by someone connected to the team. I mean, the guy is in town less than a week when Pellagrini said he was with him, and the kid was stoned."

"Could be," Murphy nodded. "He had to get the dope from somewhere."

"Doesn't that put a new light on the murder?"

"Not necessarily! Majors had money. Drug dealers usually don't bite the hand that feeds them. Why would his dealer kill him?"

"From what I learned about Majors, lots of reasons. Majors might have slept with the guy's wife or girlfriend – and now we know that he could have slept with some guy. And I'm only suggesting that because he was stoned the second day he was in town, the dealer was someone that he met right away."

Murphy cringed. "It's a long shot, but if you give me your notebook on the employees, I'll run a check on all of those who traveled to Spring Training. You know, the supporting staff - coaches, equipment people, a medical person, the radio announcers, ground crew. Maybe one of them sells dope. And it shouldn't be a very long list. On the other hand, Penny's brother could be lying."

"Thanks, Murph. If you find out that one of them sells dope, it'll help close the case. I shoulda of thought of it before. By the way, has anyone claimed the body?"

"No one officially knows he's dead yet. Well, the team knows, but so far we kept it out of the newspapers."

"The killer knows!" I said.

"Majors was an orphan. No family, and apparently no friends accept maybe Charlie Wilson. I don't think anyone will attend his pauper's funeral. Anything else you're keeping from me?"

I shook my head. "Trust me Murph. I was never a Boy Scout, but I always wanted to eat a Brownie." I raised two fingers in the air like the Boy Scout honesty motto sign. "Boy Scouts honor. I've told you everything."

Murphy replied with his middle finger and waved me out the door.

I cabbed back to the waterfront. I was concerned about how to feel about suspecting Penny. Hell, I'd now fallen in love with her. York said that he called that second night and she had answered the phone. *Is she a killer, or just forgetful, or a liar?* I wondered. *She certainly has the best motive if the monster did come back the second night and raped her. Did the girl I made love to last night still have her cherry? If she did and I broke it ---? No blood! She said it hurt, but she never yelped. So I assumed ---? Maybe she lied to me.*

I flipped a grubby panhandler a dime and hopped onto the houseboat deck. An imagined stab in the gut told me that something wasn't right. The front door stood wide open, normally okay on a hot day - but when you're acting as a bodyguard, and had left explicit instructions to keep the door closed and locked – no! Uncle Bill knew better.

I listened! I heard nothing but waves and gulls. I slowly approached the front door and poked my head inside. The first thing I saw was Bill's wheelchair laying sideways in the middle of the room, the backrest broken into two pieces. My eyes quickly circuited the room. Bill lay next to the telephone in a pool of blood. I jumped to his side, felt his skinny neck and sighed relief as I detected a pulse. Blood was oozing from the back of Bill's head as though someone had hit him with a blunt object. I picked him up and placed him on the sofa, and then placed a cold washcloth over the bruise to stop the bleeding. "Penny, Penny," I then called out, almost knowing that I wouldn't receive an answer. I quickly checked the bedrooms and bathroom to no avail. Penny was missing! I dialed an ambulance, and then Murphy.

Within five minutes the ambulance arrived and had covered Bill's face with an oxygen mask. "He's a tough old codger," the medic said as he gently positioned Bill on a stretcher. "Looks like he'll be okay, but a very large headache."

I let out a long breath. "He's always a large headache. But thanks! Can I ride in the ambulance to the hospital?"

"Relative?"

"He's my uncle."

"Hop aboard, nephew," the medic said.

My worst fear had been realized. Or I assumed that it had. Penny had been kidnapped by Nash's bookie boss.

CHAPTER TWENTY

BOSTON POST HEADLINES 1946

FRANKIE LAINE RECORDS *THAT'S MY DESIRE*

30 MILLION PEOPLE CLOSE TO DYING OF STARVATION IN CHINA

I USED THE HOSPITAL PAYPHONE to put in a call to Wayne. No one answered. I then sat in Bill's hospital room planning my next move. *Murphy? No! Police work is too slow and bureaucratic. Wayne? Yes! He knows that the fastest way to a solution is a straight line, even if something crooked has to be done to follow it. But I'll have to wait 'till Bill wakes up before I can even begin looking for Penny.*

After an hour, Bill stirred, opened his red-rimmed eyes and recognized me. "Johnny? Johnny? Is that you Johnny? Shit! I'm so sorry. Where's Penny?"

I wiped away erupting perspiration from the old man's forehead. "Calm down, Bill. You're going to be okay. Want to tell me what happened?"

"Big bruisers! Two of 'em! Never knocked! Just walked in and grabbed Penny by the throat. Asked her where Nash was. She said she didn't know. So one of them took a blackjack out of his pocket and threatened to hit me with it if she didn't tell."

"She should've told," I said, realizing that I'd made a mistake by not advising her to squeal. "Nash was a piece of shit and deserves whatever those hoodlums have in store for him. He isn't worth protecting."

"I think she thought that you wanted her to keep quiet," Bill mumbled. "Got anything I can drink."

"Water?"

"Are you kidding? You know what W.C. Fields said about water, which he refused to drink?"

"No Bill, why didn't W. C. Fields drink water?"

"Because fish fuck in it."

I had been brought up on most of Uncle Bill's corny jokes, but hadn't heard that one, so I genuinely laughed.

"You must be feeling better, Bill," I said and handed him an orange that I brought with me from the houseboat. "This will give you healthy vitamin C."

Bill smiled and began sucking.

"Tell me what happened when she refused to talk?" I asked.

"They worked me over with a blackjack."

I wiped Bill's forehead again. "I can see that. And I promise they'll pay for that decision."

Bill tried to sit up, fell back and said, "But I got in a few choice words about their nationality and appearance, Johnny. You would've been proud of me."

"Yeah, you're good at that Bill. And I'm sure they thought it was funny, too. That's why you got that big bump on your head. By the way, what was their nationality - as though I can't guess?"

"They were the same two mugs that were with Nash at the racetrack. Catalano and Rizzo!"

I pondered the scenario. "Worked with Nash! And, of course, they worked with Nash's boss. Apparently Nash took our advice and didn't tell them where he was flying the coop to. Now I wish he had."

"What are you going to do, Johnny?"

"I can wait for them to contact me for a trade of Penny for the Nash information. Or, I can beat them to the punch and find them first."

"So?"

I fluffed up my uncle's pillow, placed the old man's head gently back in place and asked. "What would you do?"

"Timeth and tideth waiteth for no maneth," Bill recited with a chuckle.

"Who the hell said that? Shakespeare? I thought you only read comic books."

Bill scratched his brow. "Yeah, maybe that's where I read it. Captain Marvel said it."

I checked with the doctor before leaving the hospital. Bill had a bad concussion, but would be fine in a few days. I then cabbed back to the houseboat and put in another call to Wayne. This time the hit man picked up. "How long will it take you to find out the name and address of Nash's boss?" I asked.

"Five minutes!"

I related the activities of the past several hours, and then said, "Make it four, please. I think I'm in love."

Not a church-goer, but an acceptor of the philosophy that some higher power created the universe, I hung up the phone and slowly folded my hands together, closed my eyes and prayed to the Creator. *I'm not asking anything for myself, Sir - just for Penny. She's only a young, innocent girl who doesn't deserve any of this crap. My guess is that You are passive and allow us all to do our own things. And I respect that. But maybe You can reach out and give me a hand in this matter. I think I need mental and physical strength to help her. I don't go to church, and I don't tithe, but I do try and do one good deed every day. Hey, if everyone did that, wouldn't the world be a helluva nice place to live? Today, I even gave that panhandler a dime - and I guess I could've given him a quarter. Well, anyway Sir, at least I've asked, and anything You can do to help will be appreciated. Amen!*

The phone rang. I checked my watch. Three minutes. "Hello," I said.

"It's Wayne! The guy's name is Cioffi. Works out of Providence. One of the Godfather's sons. Tough son-of-a-bitch. They're all connected down there. The Family controls a bank, a racetrack, a construction company, the mayor, and maybe even the police chief. Has anyone contacted you?"

"Not yet! Do you think they will?"

"In a kidnapping they usually contact someone. Butch is in jail, so you're the next best bet. We can wait, or go after them."

"I prayed to God," I admitted, hesitantly.

"Yeah? So what good did that do?" Wayne sounded sarcastic.

Maybe Wayne's not religious, I told myself. "I thought I might find some answers."

"You and a lot of other religious fanatics. But let's get serious now. Penny's life might be in the balance. How many guns do you carry?"

"Usually none, but sometimes one. Why?"

"Where do you holster it?"

"Under my left arm. How many do you carry?"

"Three?"

"Three? Where the hell do you carry three?"

"Ever notice that I wear cowboy boots?"

"Yeah!"

"I have one in my boot – a tiny six-shooter. Then I have one in a holster on my belt on the small of my back."

"And the third?"

Wayne cackled like a chicken laying a fat egg. "I'd rather not say. But I'll bring you a pair of boots and two more pistols. How about a size ten?"

"Good guess," I said. "Ten D."

"It wasn't a guess. I borrowed your spikes once. They fit perfect and I'm a ten. The third gun is also very small and carries only one bullet. You've seen them in those western movies. The hostesses in the saloons carry them in their ruffles. Very dainty!"

"And you won't tell me where I'm gonna conceal it?"

"Just wear tight underpants, don't fart, and you'll be fine. I'll pick you up in an hour. We're off to Providence to see the wizard of this caper and change the script."

CHAPTER TWENTY-ONE

BOSTON POST HEADLINES 1946

AVERAGE WORKING MAN'S WAGES PER YEAR: $2,500

A DOZEN EGGS PRICE UP TO 29 CENTS

WAYNE HAD CHECKED SOME OLD NEWSPAPER CLIPPINGS on bad guys and found this one about Cioffi. I read aloud as Wayne drove. "Paul Cioffi was born in Federal Hill, Rhode Island, 1900. He is the first son of the head of The Family, Godfather Robert Cioffi. Paul has two younger brothers and a sister. Paul is in charge of all bookmaking activities and prostitution. He is heir to his father's position. Godfather Robert is currently serving ten years in a Massachusetts state penitentiary for income tax evasion. Paul is married with two children attending exclusive private schools. He makes his office in a modest Italian restaurant located in the center of Providence's financial business district. He's known for having a violent temper."

"There's the restaurant," Wayne announced as we pulled into a parking lot next to a large office building. The restaurant was on the first floor. A gold plated sign over the front entrance read - The Lean Tower.

Clever, I thought.

Wayne shot a glance at me. "Got your guns in place. They'll frisk us as soon as they find out who we are."

I uncomfortably changed my seating position - something I'd done several times during the two-hour drive from Boston. "Yeah! I'm fine."

"Let me do the talking," Wayne said. "I've actually met this lowlife and put away two of his associates."

I raised my eyebrows. "Away? Like way away? Or in prison?"

Wayne parked, flipped the attendant the keys, winked at me, and said - "Way away."

We both dressed in dark colored, three–piece suits, blending in with the style of the day for businessmen who would be expected to populate this section of the city. We entered the restaurant that appeared like any other middle class eatery. Nothing too fancy! The maitre de, a middle-aged, short, tuxedoed dressed man greeted us with a smile and offered to seat us. My wristwatch read noon, so the midweek business crowd was beginning to arrive.

"Booth or table," the maitre de asked with a toothy smile - the smell of tobacco and tomato strong.

Wayne spoke in a firm tone, his voice lower and harsher than I had ever heard on the Park League baseball diamond.

"Need to see Cioffi. Name's Dark! He'll see us!"

The maitre de head-to-toed each man, turned and waved to the far end of the room. A large football player looking man nodded and approached. He wore a fancy three-piece suit that didn't quite fit. Too small! His muscles appeared to have muscles.

"Follow me," he said in a monotone.

We followed him across the restaurant floor into a bustling kitchen and through a door into a fairly large back room. The gorilla turned and asked, again in monotone, "Which one of youse is Dark?"

I stalled for a split second, and then raised my hand.

Quick like a cat, the big man grabbed my armpit, squeezed, reached in with his other hand and removed a gun.

"Got any more of these, bud?"

I took a deep breath, shot a look at Wayne, and said, "Just that one. And I got a license for it."

The man turned his attention to Wayne, sized him up, and then asked, "And who are you, Mac?"

Wayne moved forward and puffed out his chest. The gorilla had about four inches in height and forty pounds in weight and muscle on him. "I'm to him what you are to Cioffi. Want my piece?"

The big man backed away a few inches. "Just doin' my job, Mac. Just doin' what I'm told. If you wanna see Mr. Cioffi, you gotta be unarmed."

Wayne reached behind his back and pulled out his gun from its holster, and then removed the smaller one from his boot.

"Give him your boot gun, too, Johnny," he said.

I followed suit.

The goon pocketed all guns.

"Follow me, boys," he said. "I think he's been expecting Mr. Dark."

It was a posh room, fur rugs tacked to the walls, a mirror on the ceiling and floor. The man seated behind a large oak desk was partly bald, well built, resembled George Raft, a tough-guy movie star. Two lovely naked ladies were pampering him - one manicuring his nails - the other trimming his remaining hair. There were no chairs in the room - just big silk pillows.

"Pull up a finger and sidown, boys," Cioffi said with a chuckle.

The big henchman laughed.

Cioffi grinned. "Just kidding around, boys. I like jokes. Hear the one about the cross-eyed seamstress? Couldn't mend straight. Like menstruate. Get it?"

The goon laughed louder.

Wayne and I remained somber.

Cioffi shook his head. "You boys got no sense of humor. Laughter is the best medicine in the world. Didn't you guys know that? Laugh and the world laughs with you. Cry and you cry alone. I made that up."

Wayne and I sank our butts into two large pillows on the floor in front of Cioffi – maybe ten feet from his desk. In the ceiling mirror we could see that three other large men stood in different corners of the room - all armed with pistols.

Wayne started the conversation. "We came to pick up Penny. Any problem with that?"

Cioffi leaned forward and squinted. "Do I know you? You somehow seem familiar."

Wayne shook his head. "No one knows me, mister. So let me tell you again - we're here for Penny."

Cioffi waved the two naked girls away. "Thanks girls! Tomorrow! Same time, same station."

The girls exited the room, smiling at Wayne and me.

Cioffi spoke in an agitated tone. "Who the fuck do you two assholes think you are coming into my restaurant without an invitation?"

Wayne mind-measured the distance between him and the guard at the door, and then the three goons. He and I each had a one-bullet gun up our butt creases. I still had my knife. The odds sucked!

"We come in peace," Wayne said. "We just want the girl."

"And you know what I want," Cioffi barked.

"We know," Wayne answered. "And we're willing to give you that information."

Cioffi's eyes widened. "And why didn't you tell me that right away?"

"Because then we would have missed all your humor."

Cioffi frowned, realizing that Wayne was making fun of him. "Okay Mac, on with it. Where's Nash hiding out?"

I started to talk and Wayne lightly placed his hand over my mouth. "We'd like to see Penny first. I'm sure you understand."

Cioffi nodded and waved a hand to the first big goon who left the room and returned within thirty seconds, Penny in front of him, naked as the other two girls had been.

"Jesus," I whispered and started to get up. "What the hell is going on here?"

"Hold your horses," Wayne warned in a low voice and grabbed the back of my pants. "She's not likely to try an escape without clothes. It's more humane than tying her up in rope or chains."

Penny broke away from the goon's grip and ran into my outstretched arms. "Johnny, oh Johnny, it's so great to see you. I'm so frightened."

I was standing, removed my suit jacket and placed it around Penny's shoulders as she cuddled beside me. We sat down next to Wayne on two large pillows.

"Did they hurt you?" Wayne whispered.

"Not really! My feelings maybe - and I don't feel very good walking around naked. But they fed me well. No one abused me."

Wayne stood up and approached Cioffi's desk. "Nash went to Key West. I don't know his address, but I do know he made a bet at Narragansett and left town with a lot of money. I strongly advised him to pay you."

Cioffi squinted. "The prick still owes me and I always get paid – one way or another." He reached into his top drawer and removed a pistol. He aimed it at Wayne's midsection. "So now you've told me what I want to know. Why should I release any of you? Do you think I'm a fool?"

Wayne began to scratch his ass. "Hemorrhoids! I got a bad case. Very uncomfortable! Ever hear of Judge Stamos from Boston?"

Cioffi blinked! "Yeah! Of course I've heard of him. He sent a few of my people away, including my father. And a few others have mysteriously disappeared I think because of him. Why? Do you know him?"

"My mentor, one could say." Wayne slowly reached in the back of his pants, made a face, scratched and removed his small one-shot pistol. "I got two reasons that you'll let us go. One is a letter addressed and mailed to Judge Stamos from me. He only opens it if he doesn't see me tomorrow. The second reason is this." He pointed the little pistol at Cioffi's head. "One shot! But that's all I'll need to put you to sleep - forever. So, what do you say, asshole? Can we be on our way? If you don't find Nash, you know where to find us."

Cioffi's hand visibly shook at the word asshole.

I'm shocked that Wayne dared call him an asshole, I thought to myself. *That word is famous for really pissing people off.*

Cioffi leaned forward, frowned, and said in a gruff tone, "No one dares to insult me in my own joint. Who the fuck do you think you are?" He aimed his big pistol at Wayne's midsection.

Wayne didn't blink. "Are you going to pull the trigger, asshole, or just fiddle with it like it's your little penis?"

I decided that it must have been time to start rubbing the lower part of my leg, my fingers just inches from my nine-inch knife.

Cioffi began to smile. "I ain't falling for any of your shit, Mac. Don't you think I know you're trying to fuck with me? Take the damn girl and get the hell outta here. If I don't find Nash, you'll be hearing from me."

Wayne stood up and backed away from the desk, keeping his little gun aimed at Cioffi. "Come on Johnny, get Penny and let's get out of here."

I helped Penny to her feet, and the three of us backed towards the door.

All of a sudden all hell broke loose. One of the trigger-happy guards in a far corner raised his gun and shot the little pistol right out of Wayne's hand. Cioffi quickly fired a shot into Wayne's chest. I grabbed my knife and flung it across the room, maybe thirty feet. Bulls-eye into the neck of the shooter. I then reached into the back of my pants, removed the small pistol from my ass crack and fired at Cioffi. A small hole formed itself in the center of the shocked man's face. He instantly fell forward in a pool of blood gathering on his desk.

The remaining three hoods were momentarily dazed seeing their leader killed.

I pushed Penny onto the floor and threw an arm-full of pillows on top of her, and then quickly rushed behind Cioffi's desk, fumbling around for the gang leader's pistol. Finding it still clutched in the dead man's hand, I wrenched it free, jumped up and fired a single shot into the closest guard's chest – and then spun and fired on the man nearest to the door. The final guard dove onto the floor and grabbed Penny.

She screamed!

Wayne lay about six feet away - not moving!

"I'll kill the bitch," the guard growled, now lying on the floor with Penny as a shield. "And your life ain't worth a plug nickel after this mess."

"What do you want me to do?" I asked from behind the desk.

"Throw out the gun and follow it."

"Are you crazy?"

"I'll kill the girl."

"You'll kill the girl anyway."

"What do you suggest? I don't want to die. I ain't no hero."

"Neither am I. Let me take the girl out of here and I don't know anything. Tell everyone that Wayne killed your boss. I'm not a cop. I just came to save her life."

The man paused for a long moment, and then said, "Okay! Come on out from behind the desk. I'll let her go."

I pondered his situation. Cioffi's gun appeared too light. I looked down and spun the chamber. *Six empty slots,* I informed myself. *Fuck me! If the goon is loyal to the family, Penny and I are dead meat.* I surveyed the room. Cioffi's body lay directly beside me, a small hole in the corpse's forehead. Blood still spilt down over his eyes, over his cheeks, and onto his shirt collar. Wayne hadn't moved since he was drilled in the chest. The gorilla who had led them into the room still twitched by the door, his eyes occasionally opening and closing, and my knife protruding from his neck. The other goon near the door appeared stone cold dead. My remaining adversary was hiding behind Penny. She froze in the middle of the room, naked. I could almost count the goose bumps. I glanced up at the mirrored ceiling, something that the enemy obviously hadn't thought of. If he had he might have noticed that I was defenseless. I no longer held Cioffi's empty gun.

I looked over at Wayne whose hands began to ever so slightly move. He had the midget gun in one bleeding hand, and in the other he seemed to be fumbling in his pocket for something. *Does he have another bullet?* I wondered.

Penny sobbed. "Please, please Johnny, I want to go home. Do something, please."

I felt the back of my neck heat up with anger. I had been around long enough to know that if I allowed my emotions to dictate my next moves, Penny and I would probably never leave the restaurant or Rhode Island alive. I continued to watch Wayne fumbling in his back pocket. He lay directly to my left and the goon's right. To the goon's view, Wayne appeared motionless. Unless, of course, he looked up into the mirror.

A simple glance at the mirrored ceiling would have told a different story.

"Let the girl go and I'll throw out my gun," I called and picked up Cioffi's pistol.

"Throw out your gun first and then I'll let the girl go," the goon responded.

It looked like Wayne had found a bullet and was blindly flubbing it into the small gun barrel. I held my breath.

Wayne's midget gun dropped on the floor.

Shit! Did the enemy hear? No reaction came!

Wayne slowly picked up the gun in one hand and appeared to place the bullet into the single chamber. He then took a big gamble. He turned his head and stared up at the ceiling mirror and slowly and silently mouthed words aimed at me: "THROW

OUT CIOFFI'S GUN, THEN STAND UP." Blood was dripping from his lips.

I stared up into the mirror and sent back a puzzled frown, so Wayne mouthed the words again. T H R O W O U T T H E F U C K I N' G U N A N D S T A N D U P.

I analyzed the angle of Penny and her captor. Wayne would have a perfect shot if the goon turned his head towards me away from Penny. And he probably would do that if I stood up and threw out Cioffi's gun. He would then probably shoot. I was dead meat if Wayne missed. I recalled the day at the races. *I never gamble,* Wayne had said. And then he'd said, *When I do something, I'm positive it'll work out. Would he now gamble on Penny's life?* I asked myself. *Would he gamble on my life? Only if he knew for sure it would work.*

"Here comes the g - gun, mister," I stuttered and stood up straight, becoming an easy target for the shooter. "Now let the girl go. Okay?"

"Yeah bud, okay. Anything you say."

I flipped Cioffi's pistol over the front of the desk out into the middle of the floor, maybe two or three feet from Penny.

Cioffi's man took a step forward, leaned over and picked it up, chuckled, and placed it in his pocket. He then lifted Penny to her feet, ogled her naked figure, and surprisingly handed her my suit jacket. She quickly slipped it on. The goon pushed her in front of him with one hand, and held his own gun in the other. He slowly approached the desk. As they passed the motionless body of Wayne, only six feet away, I heard a small pop. The goon grabbed his neck as blood spurted forth like a leak in a Holland dike. Apparently Wayne had shot the gangster in the juggler vein. No gamble there! Instant death! The goon tumbled in a heap in front of Penny. She screamed, ran to me and threw her arms around me.

"Is it over?" she cried into my chest.

I walked towards Wayne. I turned him over onto his back. The hit man's eyes were wide open and staring. His closed mouth carried a slight grin. I knelt beside my friend and felt his pulse, and then his heart. "Guess he made his last hit a home run for our team," I whispered to Penny.

I quickly cased the room, retrieved my knife, and spied a back door. "Give me a minute to restage this mess and then let's get going, doll. I don't think we're going to be very popular around here after they discover this mess."

CHAPTER TWENTY-TWO

BOSTON POST HEADLINES 1946

**FAMOUS PEOPLE BORN:
DONALD TRUMP,
STEVEN SPEILBERG,
GEORGE BUSH,
CHER**

**WAR CRIMES TRIALS
HELD IN TOKYO**

I DROPPED PENNY OFF AT HER APARTMENT. "I'm going to call Murphy," I told her. "Tell him as much as I think he should know, and then maybe play blackboard games. I think that the true facts of what happened today should stay with the two remaining witnesses. You and me! Agree?"

She nodded. "Do you have to leave me just yet, Johnny? I don't feel so good." She was shivering all over.

"Just a little while longer, doll, and then we can spend a lot of time together. Lock the door and I'll be back before you know it. Trust me, there's no one left to worry about."

It was mid-afternoon and Murphy was waiting for me at the houseboat.

"Got your call," he said. "You said you had some important stuff to tell me about the Majors' case, and you mentioned the wise guys in Rhode Island? I didn't quite figure how the two were related."

I fired up a Chesterfield and used the match to light the pot bellied stove in the middle of the room. Sometimes, in late August, the harbor brought breezes that reminded inhabitants of the coming New England Fall. The radio hummed in the background, the Red Sox now on the road playing in Detroit.

Murphy turned the sound dial down. "Okay! I'm ready. What have you been keeping from me?"

"I'm not sure I can tell you everything."

The phone rang.

I answered and frowned. I talked for less than a minute and then handed the phone to Murphy. "It's for you. Do you know Judge Stamos?"

"Doesn't everyone?"

"Not me! Heard of him! Never met him!"

Murphy grabbed the phone, said a few words, and then listened. He shook his head as he hung up. "Are you sure you don't know the judge?"

"I told you. I never met the man."

"Well, somehow he knows you. He doesn't want you to tell me anything until he talks to you in person. Do you know what it's about?"

I shrugged. "I guess it's about what happened earlier today in Rhode Island. But I'm surprised th ---."

Murphy waved his hand for me to shut up. "I'll give you directions to the judge's house. He wants to meet you there in an hour. Private stuff, I guess. He's a pretty influential guy. If he says he wants to see you, you see him."

"Where does he live?"

"Newton - about 45 minutes from here. Maybe 30 minutes if I blow my siren."

"Then you can blow it. First, let's play on the blackboard."

I stood up and walked to the board carrying two erasers. I clapped them together and coughed in all the white dust I had created. "This was my chore in the fifth grade," I said with a smile and started by erasing some of the names, leaving: FRANK MAJORS, 20, DECEASED – MURDERED. BAD HABITS: 1. DOPE 2. WOMEN. SUSPECTS: 1. RONALD NASH. 2. PENNY'S BROTHER. 3. ___? POSSIBLE CLUES: SCISSORS OWNED BY PENNY. 1945 – LAST YEAR'S PLAYERS NO LONGER WITH TEAM: 1. EDDIE LAKE. 2. PAUL CAMBELL. 3. JOHNNY LAZOR. 4. CHARLIE WILSON.

"Why are you erasing all the currant ballplayers?" Murphy asked.

"Because they're all innocent. I've investigated and that's my decision. You know this procedure. Put up all the possibilities, and then start eliminating them one by one. Whoever is left is the killer. Easy! Right? Any fool can play."

Murphy shrugged, walked to the icebox and removed a cold scotch bottle, flipped off the top and took a long swig. "Will Bill mind?"

"Not if he don't know," I said and took a piece of chalk and wrote: CHARLIE WILSON. He was now listed twice, so I erased both.

Murphy shook his head. "I thought he was our new suspect."

"He cried real tears. Killers don't do that. Do they?"

Murphy shrugged. "Us cops don't have the luxury of the blackboard game. We have to come up with courtroom acceptable proof."

I put my pointer finger to my chin and tapped. "How about this Bull Brown guy? Looks like he's got a boner for Wilson and Wilson had a boner for Majors. Isn't jealousy one of the prime motives for murder?"

Murphy nodded, so I wrote: BULL BROWN, WRESTLER.

"I notice you didn't even put up Penny's name," Murphy said and placed the bottle back into the icebox.

"Let's go to the judge's house and find out what he wants," I suggested. "Maybe he knows something we don't."

"He wants you to come alone," Murphy said. "Take my squad car. Use the siren if you want. I'll wait here."

CHAPTER TWENTY-THREE

BOSTON POST HEADLINES 1946

FAMOUS PEOPLE BORN: SYLVESTOR STALLONE, DOLLY PARTON, JIMMY BUFFET, TED BUNDY

BBC TELEVISION SERVICE BEGINS IN USA

JUDGE STAMOS'S HOUSE LOOKED MORE LIKE AN INN. It was situated on several acres fronting Commonwealth Avenue in a plush section of Newton, fifteen miles West of Boston. The famous annual 27 - mile marathon passes by his front lawn every year in April. He chose not to ever run in it, or to run anywhere else. His major exercise was Curling at the plush Brookline Country Club. He owned a bunch of small medals on his beret to prove it. A long driveway squirreled its way through Oaks and Maples to the front steps. Wooden pillars reminded me of Tara in the popular movie, Gone With the Wind. A Negro servant met the police car, opened the door and reached for the key. "Judge Stamos is waiting for you on the porch, mistah. I'll bring your car around when you're ready to leave."

I forced a smile, feeling quite anxious as to why the judge ordered my presence. *Did he know about Wayne's meeting with Cioffi?* I wondered. *Did he know that Cioffi was dead? Did he know that Wayne was dead? Is he going to blame me?*

The judge was younger, or appeared younger than I had imagined. *Aren't all judges old men with white hair?* I asked myself. The only judge I was familiar with was Mickey Rooney's father in the popular Andy Hardy movie series. He was old with white hair.

Stamos was sixty plus, sported a thin Clark Gable mustache, and a tanned complexion. He could have passed for an English aristocrat, or a leading man in a Broadway play. His natty three-piece suit covered an athletic build and I immediately wondered if the court official had ever played baseball.

We gripped hands as the judge remained seated. I pulled up a wicker chair and sat. I noticed the morning newspaper opened to the sports page and a story about the Red Sox climbing closer to the pennant. I suddenly wondered if I'd qualify for a World Series ring. *Hmm! Nice!*

"I attended the game where you got your hit, my boy," the judge said in a gravelly voice. He stuffed a pipe bowl with tobacco and began lighting it up, puffing and inhaling.

"Ever play the game, sir?" I asked. "You look quite athletic."

The judge smiled behind a pipe smoke cloud. "Actually, I was quite a good hitter at Nobles and Greenough School in Dedham. Then I spent four years on the Harvard diamond. I always had that dream of playing for the Red Sox. Back when I played they were located on Huntington Avenue. Fenway wasn't built until 1912. How did you feel getting your one at bat?"

I rubbed my forehead while pondering the answer. "I think I would have melted like the wicked witch of the West if the rookie catcher hadn't revealed what the pitcher was going to throw. I think even the ump wanted me to get a hit."

The judge raised his eyebrows. "You mean they actually helped you? I didn't know that about baseball. That shows a certain amount of compassion. I like that."

I smiled and nodded in agreement. "The game was out of reach. The catcher told me about the first time he was up at the plate and how scared shitless he'd been."

"And?" The judge leaned forward.

"He admitted that he struck out on three pitches."

"How did it feel when you saw the ball hit the wall?"

"Well, I got this gimpy knee, and I began reciting short prayers that I wouldn't fall down before reaching first base. Funny thing how a non-religious person will ask God for favors when in distress."

The judge let out a chuckle. "Yeah! I've done that before. I don't know if prayers work – but they certainly don't hurt."

"Ted really helped, too," I nodded and added."

"How was that?"

"Told me to keep my right elbow up."

"I guess he ought to know. He may win the Triple Crown this year. Certainly the Most Valuable Player award."

I leaned back in my chair, lit a Chesterfield, and puffed out a small ring. "You didn't invite me all the way to your Newton estate to listen to me talk baseball, did you sir?"

The judge shook his head. "Wayne told me you were a smart and honest detective. And no, I didn't invite you here to talk baseball, but to talk about my deceased employee. Do you want to tell me what went down at Cioffi's restaurant? And remember, I'm an experienced judge and will know when you're telling me anything less than the truth."

The Negro servant approached the porch table and asked, "Refreshments anyone?"

The judge glanced at his pocket watch attached to a gold chain. "I guess it's close enough to that time. I'll have the usual, Manton. What about you Mr. Dark?"

"Beer will do." *This guy reminds me of Yawkey and the yardarm,* I thought to myself.

The judge pulled his wicker chair closer. "Did Wayne tell you what services he performed for me?"

I hesitated, contemplating a lie. "He mentioned something about it. But if he hadn't helped me, Mr. Yawkey's secretary would still be a kidnap victim of Paul Cioffi - or dead."

"I've been in contact with the Providence police. They say that it appears as though Wayne shot Mr. Cioffi and three bodyguards. Another dead guard was found with a knife wound in his neck. Is that right, my boy?"

"Would that be the best scenario, sir?"

The judge twiddled with his mustache. "Maybe yes! I haven't quite thought it all the way through. Those five people won't be missed on the face of this earth as far as I'm concerned. But we have to examine the possibility of retaliation. You must be smart enough to know that you don't walk into the Cioffi family restaurant, off five of the family members, and walk away unscathed."

"I thought about that and that's why it's important that all the blame is placed with Wayne."

"Good plan, my boy. But someone else has to know about the girl other than the five who are coffin fillers."

Manton served the drinks along with some fresh shrimp and hot sauce, and then shuffled away. The judge was drinking ice tea. *At least it looks like ice tea,* I thought.

"I felt as emotionally about Wayne as if he were my son," the judge said, his eyes beginning to moisten.

I shook my head and swigged down half of my beer.

"Tell me how it went down, please," the judge asked.

I then related the entire scene, minute-by-minute, threat-by-threat - the knife throw, and then shot by shot. "And when I realized that Wayne was dead, I quickly decided that if he became the sole killer, just maybe the Cioffi family would back off, believing the culprit had already paid his dues. I took all the guns that had been used against the family, wiped them clean and placed Wayne's prints on them. I even put his fingerprints on my knife and put it back into the dead guy's neck. Then Penny and I ducked out the back way. I guess the office must have been sound-proof because the whole time we were there no one interrupted us."

The judge daintily sipped his tea and asked, "Now tell me about the Majors' killing - everything you know and everything you suspect."

I sunk down in my chair. "I got some unsubstantiated suspicions," I said. "No real proof!"

"Stop stalling and lay it on me. I'm a big boy and I have a hot date tonight. At my time of life I pay for my companionship. It works real well. No commitments, and in the long run, believe it or not, it's a hellava lot cheaper. No divorce courts!"

I digested the sex-life philosophy lesson and decided that it wasn't all that bad. I'd known too many divorces that ended with lawyers making out much better than the couple. And I'd known too many guys who married because they thought it would be a good way to get regular sex. It reminded me of a Curly Howard line from several of the Three Stooges short subjects: *"Are you married or are you happy? Yuk, yuk, yuk."*

I brought my attention back into the room and said, "Well, this is what I think happened. Mr. Yawkey's secretary, Penny Mitchell was raped by that young punk pitcher, Stephen Majors. Who was also a bad doper."

"Wait a cotton pickin' minute, boy. What makes you think she was raped?"

"She said that he tried and couldn't get it up. Too much booze and dope."

"So? What makes you doubt her?"

I dawdled, pondered my answer, and then asked - shamefacedly, "When's the last time you slept with a virgin, sir?"

The judge hesitated, sent a puzzled expression, puffed on his pipe, and didn't answer.

"Judge?"

"I'd rather not answer. But know what you mean."

"She told me that she had never slept with her fiancée. I tended to believe that story. She's only twenty-one years old and seems very naïve. Plus, the guy sincerely wanted to marry her."

"I understand! I've been love-struck before. Too many times, I confess. But it certainly gives her a motive."

"She denied that Majors raped her, but I have good reason to believe that he went back a second night and did. And if she did have something to do with his death, I can't blame her. I admit that I don't begin to understand the opposite sex, but if I were a woman, I'd never admit to a rape. Never!"

"I've been married and divorced three times," the judge said. "Are you sure she isn't a virgin?"

At first I didn't answer. I fiddled with my cigarette, blew a few rings, and then said, "Since you're a judge, I suppose I must confess to sleeping with her one time, and she said that when I penetrated that it hurt, but she didn't yelp when it happened. So maybe she was a virgin. But maybe she wasn't. I understand that the first time it is supposed to hurt and bleed. I'm embarrassed, but sneakily checked to see if she bled and found no blood."

The judge puffed on his pipe, smiled and said, "Continue, my boy."

"She supposedly told her brother and her fiancée about the attempted rape by Majors. Her boyfriend turned out to be a bookie and a dirt-bag."

"So that gives us three suspects. And I know about Nash. He's why you ended up in Rhode Island. Right?"

I nodded and preceded to reveal the reason Mr. Yawkey had hired me in the first place. I then told the judge about Majors' Spring Training sexual antics, messing with the ball player's girlfriends and wives – and added Pellagrini's suspicion of someone connected with the team might be supplying Majors with dope. I ended the tale with the revelation of Charlie Wilson getting released, but also queer for Majors. And vice versa.

The judge's demeanor went from cracking several smiles to some serious grunts and groans as though enjoying a radio soap opera. "Wayne said you were a good peeper," he said. "So, who finally killed the fast-baller?"

"I can't tell you sir."

"What if I've already figured it out? Or should I say that Wayne figured it out and told me?"

"Nothing I can do about that sir."

"Well, actually there is. Sounds to me as though you're a loyal type of guy. Am I right?"

"You could say that."

"So was Wayne! He told me about Nash and Cioffi. It had nothing to do with him, or me, or his job, but he put his life on the line for you and your girlfriend. Do you know what the last thing he said to me was?"

I shrugged.

"He said that if he ever was taken out of the game, you would be the best pinch hitter."

I double-taked. *Should I be flattered that someone thinks I'd make a good hit man? Or is he literally talking about the Park League where Wayne and I played together on the same team?* I shivered at the first thought.

"Thanks, but no thanks, sir. I'm flattered, but I'm no murderer."

The judge leaned forward across the table and locked firmly into my eyes. "Is the man who flips the switch on the electric chair a murderer?" he asked.

"Of course not!"

"Why not?"

I mulled the question over in my now befuddled mind. "I, uh - because the convict was legally sentenced to death?"

"And why was he sentenced to death?" the judge questioned, leaning even closer.

"I guess because he deserved it? A jury said he was guilty?"

"I'd say you're on the right track. And you did kill a few of Cioffi's henchmen. Did they deserve it?"

I went silent!

The judge continued. "Now, let's investigate this hypothesis. It's one that might save your girlfriend's life - and one that might save your life. Okay, my boy?"

This guy should be a Fuller Brush salesman, I thought. *He could sell iceboxes to Eskimos.*

The judge leaned back and relit his pipe. "I figure that Majors goes back the second night to rape the girl. This time he does get it up and completes the act. He's doped up, falls asleep, her brother shows up, and they both kill him. How am I doing so far?"

I tried to shrivel up into as small a ball as I could. "Sounds plausible so far, sir."

"Or, the above happens and the brother shows up on the scene, drags the doper out and kills him. Like that better?"

I reluctantly nodded.

"Butchy boy sets up the cement shoe affair to look like a professional hit. I'm sure with the hooligans he rubs elbows with he'd heard about how the pros eliminate there foes. When he realizes that his sister is a suspect, he takes the rap. I like people like that."

I nodded. "I guess everyone has a good side. Did Wayne figure that all out?"

"Did you know Wayne was very smart and a lawyer by trade?"

I nodded again.

"I need a replacement for Wayne, and I'm willing to offer you a trade deal - your services for the guaranteed safety of you, your girlfriend, and her brother. Remember, the only people you'll be asked to flip the switch on are those heinous creeps who are deemed guilty of crimes warranting the death penalty. And, if you don't agree with the hits, you are not forced to follow through. I'm sure Wayne explained the entire program to you."

I rested my chin on my chest and didn't look up.

The judge said, "And I'm sure he told you about his salary. Eight hundred a job."

I now sat forward and narrowed my eyes at the judge. "Wayne said five hundred."

"Inflation, my boy. Inflation! I gave him a raise before the Cioffi job."

"Wait a damn minute. You mean he was on an assignment for you? I thought he was ---?"

"Come on my boy. Time to wake up to reality. Life isn't fair. It never was and never will be. You can live in a fantasy, or you can live in reality. I choose the latter. When I heard about what Wayne was into with you I figured I could kill two birds with one bullet. I've always wanted to get the Cioffi family. I can't tell you how many of those crooks have been up in front of me and got sprung by high priced, smart-ass lawyers." He puffed deeply on his pipe and watched the smoke evaporate over his head. "Hey son, when you became a cop, what oath did you take? Do you remember?"

I took The Thinker pose, and then said, "To serve and protect?"

"Right! To serve and protect! Serve the best interests of the innocent sheep who fumble around day after day assuming the shepherds are doing their job - and protecting them to the best of our ability. Letting a law-breaker go free is not protecting or serving the public. Is it?"

I had to shake my head.

The judge asked, "Do you happen to know the oath that lawyers take when they pass the bar?"

I thought for a minute, and then shrugged my shoulders.

The judge answered for me. "To search for the truth. Have you ever met a lawyer who was doing that?"

"Maybe you?"

"Not really, my boy. I was the best at what I did, but didn't get to the top searching for the truth. Sadly, those are two different animals. Every case has two lawyers, both searching to win. Sometimes the truth is buried." The judge relit his pipe and puffed for a while, allowing his lecture to sink in. "I've got a proposition for you. And as I said, it will get your girlfriend off the hook and her loser brother out of jail."

I took the final sip of my beer, sat back in my chair and advised myself to listen. *Talk is always cheap*, I told myself. *And I'll always be free to refuse. In the past five years a lot of brave people have died to keep this a free country.*

"Godfather Robert Cioffi gets released from Walpole State prison tomorrow at noon. Because of the press and other considerations, the time has been secretly changed to nine AM." The judge handed me a manila file entitled CLASSIFIED - ROBERT CIOFFI. "Thumb through this and you'll see why this animal deserves to be executed."

I opened to the first page and read where Cioffi had beaten a kid to death with a baseball bat when they were both fifteen years old. I read on for several minutes, and then looked up at the judge. "So why isn't this thug in jail for life? It looks like you had him dead to rights on his last murder with witnesses and everything."

"I did! Bully for me! But on the day before sentencing, the arresting officer came forward and recanted his original statement. He said that he'd been paid to lie."

"You were the judge. Why didn't you just throw out his entire testimony?"

"That's what I did. The jury was reconvened and came back with a 2nd degree verdict."

"Did you ever find out why the officer changed his testimony?"

"He had a wife and two little kids. Someone borrowed one of the children. I don't blame the guy for crumbling."

I rubbed my five-o'clock shadow and read a few more pages in silence. "The guy's a prick, I'll grant you that. But you finally got him on tax evasion and sent him away for ten years."

The judge smiled. "And he just got paroled after five. When he gets home and finds out his son was killed he won't rest until you and your girlfriend are pushing up daisies."

I flipped the CIOFFI file onto the floor in front of the judge. "Okay! I guess I owe it to Wayne. Just tell me what you want me to do. I'll do this one hit. But that's it! One hit! Just like my illustrious Major League Baseball career. One at bat! One hit!"

CHAPTER TWENTY-FOUR

BOSTON POST HEADLINES 1946

BOSTON CELTICS PLAY FIRST HOME GAME

22-YEAR-OLD FIDEL CASTRO, CUBAN LAW STUDENT, MAKES FIRST POLITICAL SPEECH

WHEN I RETURNED TO THE HOUSEBOAT I phoned Murphy and told him bits and pieces of the Judge Stamos visit. "He just wanted to know what had gone down in Cioffi's restaurant. So I told him."

"That's okay! He called me and told me all about it. He also told me that his office had suspected the Majors kid of buying dope from one of Cioffi's men who was now deceased – thanks to you. They got wind of the fact that Majors stiffed the dealer and so they had the pitcher killed. Case closed! The judge instructed me to let Butch Michaels go and keep mum."

"Did he explain why Butch confessed?" I asked, wondering where the judge had dreamed up the drug-selling tale.

"He didn't really have a clue what had really happened, but asked me to just drop the entire case. He said that sometimes bad things happen to good people, and that maybe Butch thought his sister had killed Majors, so decided to take the rap.

And no matter what, if Majors did rape the girl, he got what he deserved. The judge sounded like he believed in justice - one way or another."

I felt speechless for a long few moments. *Judge Stamos has more power than I realize,* I reminded myself. "Sounds reasonable to me. What about the scissors? Any fingerprints?"

"I don't know," Murphy answered. "The damn things got misplaced. So I guess we'll never really know who wielded them – or be able to prove it. Not that they had anything to do with the creep's death."

The judge is convinced that Penny killed Majors, and so was Wayne, I told myself. *I wonder! She certainly didn't carry his body under the deserted Navy Yard wharf. Butch? Yeah! Makes more sense. I'm convinced they were both in on it.*

CHAPTER TWENTY-FIVE

BOSTON POST HEADLINES 1946

WINSTON CHURCHILL FIRST TO USE PHRASE IRON CURTAIN

DR. BENJAMIN SPOCK PUBLISHES FIRST CHILD CARE BOOK

I SPENT A FITFUL EVENING WITH PENNY at her apartment. We finally agreed that she'd be more comfortable at the Kenmore Hotel. Mr. Yawkey had paid for several suites there - always available. The houseboat had proven to be unsafe. I deliberately avoided any reference to my agreement with Judge Stamos. I did tell her that her brother would be released the next day and that she and her brother should consider moving - maybe as far away as the Florida Keys – or further. We talked a lot about lots of things – baseball, high school, what makes males and females tick -avoiding anything intimate. My maleness wanted me to make love – but I had total mixed feelings about any future with a murderess. We sat in silence for several minutes. I couldn't think of anything to say. I checked my wristwatch. It was ten o'clock. We were on opposite ends of her drab couch. I glanced up at her as she seemed to suddenly perk up. I suggested. "Okay honeycakes," she answered, fluttering her eyelashes. "Let's get outta here, Sugarcake," she said. "Youll like Mr. Yawkey's pecial suite."

After I paid the cabby, Penny took my hand and I followed her through the swinging doors, across the hotel lobby into the elevator. We exited the third floor and entered room number 35. It was a large suite, two couches, a 4-poster double bed, a full bar, and a wide balconied window overlooking Kenmore Square. Penny walked to the bar and poured herself a gin on ice, and then one for me. She added tonic to both and waved for me to follow her to the bedroom. "Here, you need this to unwind," she said and handed we my glass.

I stayed on the couch, sipped and said, in a low and slow tone, "Wayne died saving you for me. He didn't have to do that."

"But it was his choice."

"I think he rewrote the script not having all the facts. And that doesn't seem fair. Does it?"

She shrugged and sat beside me. "I don't know what you're talking about. What facts didn't he know?"

"I think you know that I know."

She raised her glass to mine, clicked them together and said, "To us - two shell parts that finally linked back together, forever!" She then gulped down her drink.

I hesitated, stared into her twinkling eyes, finally smiled and took a sip. "I told you that I love you," I said softly. "But I'm afraid that it will never work between us. You remember what Uncle Bill warned you."

Penny smiled as she unbuttoned all the buttons on her shiny silk blouse, and then slipped it off over her shoulders. She reached back and unhooked her bra strap allowing the material to slide away, leaving her bare from the waist up.

I appeared hypnotized at the sensuous scene. "I - I told you that a cop's wife is no picnic," I stuttered. "And being married to someone like me is even worse. You'd never know if I'd return from work - when or how. Trust me, a wife of someone in my profession is no good for anyone - especially if we had kids. And you deserve the best life you can have, that includes the whole ball of wax - kids, a nice house with a white picket fence, a dog, cat, and a real refrigerator."

A few tears began to bubble in the corners of Penny's eyes. "But I love you, Johnny. I don't care about any of that material stuff."

"You should and would later on. I'll never change. I know that about myself." I was suddenly thinking about the judge's deal.

"But Johnny, I ---."

I placed my hand over her lips. "I know that Majors raped you and that you killed him," I said in a gentle whisper. "And I don't blame you for that."

Penny's face became stone. She pulled away and covered herself with her blouse and put a pillow over her lap. "How do you know that Majors fucked me?"

"Rudy told me that he phoned your apartment the night after you said Majors had attacked you and you'd never seen him again. Rudy called to warn you that Majors was coming over and that he was high as a kite. You answered the phone. I don't have to be a good detective to tell myself that if you answered the phone that you were home that night." I gulped down my drink, lit a Chesterfield and blew a large ring, watched it begin to float away, and then put a smaller one through it. "You lied to me, Penny."

She threw her arms around me, her eyes filled with tears, and she began hugging me. "I was afraid for my life, Johnny. I - I considered murdering him. I couldn't help it. He raped me, and I knew when he woke up he was going to try to rape me again. But I promise that I didn't kill him."

I pulled her closer. "Calm down! Please just tell me what really happened. The truth this time."

She relaxed a bit, but kept hugging. "Rudy did call me, and a few minutes later I heard the door buzzer. I clicked on the Intercom. I asked who it was. He identified himself and asked me to let him in, actually sounding sober. He said he wanted to apologize for the night before. He promised that he had cleaned up his act. He said that he was even scheduled to pitch the next Friday and that they wouldn't let him pitch if they didn't think he was clean."

"And you believed him?"

"I hesitated! But I really did. I promise! And then he kind of pleaded, sounding very harmless. He said that he adored me too much to hurt me. And Mr. Yawkey had been like a father to him. He wouldn't do anything to hurt the boss."

"So you then let him in," I said, frowning and shaking my head.

"I remember pondering that Mr. Yawkey did like him," Penny went on. "And that he could be nice when sober. And he was quite handsome. And I hadn't met you yet. So I said okay! But only for a little while. Maybe a cup of coffee. I told him that my brother was coming over later."

I wasn't enjoying the narrative. "What time was that?"

"It was past nine and I was already wearing silk pajamas, long shirt top with collar, and long pants bottoms. Nothing sexy! I told him that I'd already eaten, but I could warm up some spaghetti and meatballs if he was hungry. He was wearing a T-shirt with a Red Sox logo on the front. He also wore a pair of wrinkled corduroy pants and sneakers. He lit up a flat cigarette and puffed deeply."

"I guess he hadn't cleaned up his act," I suggested.

She shrugged. "He offered me a drag. I immediately slapped it out of his hand and yelled at him. I think I said that I was going to have to tattle to Mr. Yawkey on him, and then asked him to leave. He let out an evil laugh and said that I wouldn't have let him in if I didn't want it. He said that all dumb broads were alike. They say no - but really mean yes. I then ran over to the telephone, picked it up and began to dial my brother. Majors followed me, grabbed the phone from my hand and ripped it out of the wall. I spit in his face. He grinned and slowly wiped the saliva off his chin. And then he reached out and violently tore the shirt right off my body. I was terrified, raised my arms and tried to cover my bare breasts. I told him that my brother would show up at any moment. And then he told me."

"Told you what?"

"He yelled that my brother was a creep and didn't give a shit about me, or anyone else. And then he confessed something I didn't know and never dreamed. He said that he had met my brother the second day that he was here and that Butch had supplied him the dope. I then started to cry. I didn't want to believe him, but ---? I then ran to the couch and pulled a blanket on top of me. He followed and sat by my feet. He seemed to calm down when he told me that he never had any parents. He was brought up in an orphanage like Babe Ruth. That's where he learned to pitch. That's also where he learned to take dope. He smoked his first toke when he was ten years old. I actually started to feel sorry for him when he gently slid over beside me and placed his hand on my blanket-covered knee. My breasts were still hidden. He said in a pleading, whining voice that that he wasn't a monster. He just wanted a chance to be a nice, regular guy. I remember quickly moving away, wrapping my arms around my knees and suggesting he go back to the hotel and we could forget any of the evening ever happened. His face took on an appearance of sadness and he asked if I would really do something nice for him and forgive him. I recall nodding - actually thinking he was being honest. But his demeanor suddenly changed. His voice raised and he said that he was going to screw me hard, go back to the hotel, stop drugs, and pitch for Mr. Yawkey. He said that the ball was in my court. Make love to him and he'd turn over a new leaf. Damn! I was shocked and frightened out of my wits. I jumped off the couch, the blanket flying away. I ran toward the front door. He followed, roughly caught me, dragged me back to the couch, ripped off my pajama bottoms and proceeded to complete what he had attempted to do the night before. I screamed as loud as possible that he was hurting me. He grabbed the end of the blanket and stuffed it into my mouth and told me that it was supposed to hurt the first time and that it didn't hurt him.

When he was done he rolled off of me onto the floor, lay there for a few minutes displaying a wide smile, lit a flat cigarette, puffed for a while, and then I heard snores. I carefully left the couch, made my way into the bathroom, showered hot for a long time, and finally turned on the cold. I soaped myself again, and then turned off the water. I dried myself, scrubbing so hard my skin turned pink. I threw on a robe and returned to the living room. He was still asleep. Knowing him, I figured that he'd want to have sex with me again when he woke up. I recall checking the clock. Eleven! He had ripped the phone out of the wall. Luckily, I have two phones – one in the bedroom. I dialed Nash's number and waited. It rang several times. No answer! I then thought of calling the police, but didn't know what to tell them? Would I say that Majors had dropped by the previous night and tried to rape me, failed, and then I let him come back tonight? I didn't think that was a believable story. So I dialed my brother's number, and found no answer there either. I then searched around the room for some kind of weapon. I had taken a course in high school on sewing and recently started learning the art of quilting. The quilting kit sat next to my sewing machine. I checked its contents. Spools of thread, balls of yarn, needles, and a large silver pair of eight-inch scissors! I went back to the living room where Majors lay naked on the floor next to the couch on top of a blanket. He snored and wore a small grin. I took my lipstick out of my purse and walked over to his sleeping form, leaned down and marked a red spot close to his left nipple. My high school biology class had taught me where the organs of the human body were located. I stared down at his innocent face. He never moved. So I took the scissors and lightly scratched the spot where I had marked. It drew a bit of blood, but surprisingly he didn't wake up. I swear if he had I would have driven the scissors into his heart. I sat there for about five minutes, and then went into my bedroom, locked the door behind me, and tucked myself under the covers – the scissors neatly hidden under my pillow. As far as I know my bother never showed up. About an hour later I woke up and poked my head out into the living room and called, scissors in my hand. There was no answer. And that's it. All of it! The truth! I promise!"

Penny started crying. "I didn't kill him. I didn't kill him, and I'm sorry I lied to you."

I gently ran my fingers through her hair. "You did the right thing at the time, but you shouldn't have left your brother out to dry when he confessed. I don't think he did it either. After the body was found he must have thought somehow that you did it. The truth would have been the right thing when he was arrested. The truth to me and the truth to the police."

"And it would have become a scandal," she said and began shivering. "You're right, I was protecting Mr. Yawkey and the team. Loyalty! You know about loyalty."

"I do!"

Her tears were pouring out uncontrollably. "Please Johnny, believe me. Help me! I'm sorry for what I did, and I'm more sorry that I lied to you."

She threw off her blouse and pillow and stood up directly in front of me. She was shivering all over.

I picked her up, carried her into the bedroom, and gently lay her down on the bed.

She smiled, lay back and spread her legs - very wide.

An evening breeze filtered through the curtains from an open window. The street noises seemed to be playing some kind a nighttime auto/trolley/ pedestrian tune.

I felt a churning in my stomach and an ache in my heart. I also felt a strong ache someplace else - the second brain of every man that is usually acted upon out of animal instinct. *I'm a red blooded adult male,* I told myself. *I suppose I can battle with my personal feelings tomorrow.*

My flesh was tingling, and I was in love. So I reacted!

Neither of us kept score as to how many times we satisfied each other during the night. We slept, played, slept, played - never talking very much about anything heavy - like marriage, or even living together - but we did agree that we would love each other forever. Shell parts reunited!

CHAPTER TWENTY-SIX

BOSTON POST HEADLINES 1946

NINE SPOKANE WESTERN LEAGUE BALLPLAYERS DIE IN BUS CRASH

ALL MAJOR LEAGUE BASEBALL GAMES PLAYED AT NIGHT FOR FIRST TIME

I LEFT THE HOTEL EARLY WHILE PENNY SLEPT. I was wearing the boots that Wayne had given me. They held the small pistol that I had carried in my butt crack during the Cioffi affair. I checked in at the Mass. General Hospital. Uncle Bill was coming along fine. My next stop was the houseboat. A long, sleek, black limousine awaited my arrival. On the front seat sat a small suitcase. I opened it revealing a black chauffeur's uniform - including cap. I also found a black, false mustache that I immediately attached and glanced at myself in the vehicle mirror. I didn't know if I resembled Adolph Hitler or Groucho Marx. Underneath all the paraphernalia were eight crisp one hundred dollar bills.

Judge Stamos had drawn me a road map from Boston to Walpole State Prison, and then to a large piece of land the judge owned in the Miles Standish State Forest located in Plymouth.

I was waiting outside the prison gates at nine sharp.

Two guards escorted the released prisoner to the front door, patted him on the back, and then waved as he walked into the parking lot - a free man. He was maybe sixty years old, quite short, and sported a full head of gray hair. He wore blue dungarees and a white collared shirt, no tie, and no jacket. He carried a beat-up looking brown suitcase. It was a hot day.

I motioned to the man and proceeded to open the back door. The man's eyes circuited the parking lot, and seeing only the one means of transportation, followed my directions.

"Got a name, son?" Cioffi asked as he climbed into the back seat.

"John Doe," I mumbled. "The boys thought you'd get a kick out of coming home first class."

Cioffi lit up a long cigar.

I coughed and pushed a button that closed a window between the back and front seat, keeping out the smoke. The judge had supplied the back seat with magazines, coffee, and a bottle of scotch - the hoodlum's favorite brand.

The trip was relatively quiet of any conversation. When Cioffi asked a question, I either pretended that the radio blocked out the sound, or that I was just hard or hearing. After a half hour, Cioffi gave up trying to chitchat.

The judge's Plymouth property was located deep in the State Forest. It was an old farm, well fenced and gated. I followed the map as best I could and only got lost a few times. Fortunately, Cioffi napped most of the trip after several scotch drags. He never noticed that we had left the main drag and we were traveling on dirt roads.

I pulled up in front of a large wooden gate. I quietly got out of the limo and unlatched the lock.

Cioffi still slept!

When we reached the badly-in-need-of-repairs farmhouse I parked the limo, got out of the front seat and opened the back door. "We're here Mr. Cioffi. Wake up! You're home!"

Cioffi shook his head, blinked his eyes, and stared out into the wooded area.

"What the hell?" he uttered. "Where the hell are we?"

"Your final resting place, sir," I answered. "Follow me."

Cioffi begrudgingly followed me through a small area of Evergreens into a clearing that featured a sundry of unmarked gravestones.

"What the hell is this place, bud? A pet cemetery?"

I perused the area, never having seen it before. I noticed that one shallow grave had already been dug - maybe four feet deep, six feet long, and four feet wide.

Cioffi, suddenly realizing his fate, turned and began running towards the woods.

I pulled a new nine-inch knife from its resting place next to my sock, aimed and threw. It whizzed past Cioffi's ear and stuck into a tree trunk about five yards in front him.

Shit! I never miss, I told myself. *I must be getting old. Who wrote this damn script?*

Cioffi stopped in his tracks, turned and faced me. "Can we deal?" he asked in a pleading voice. "I can grease your palm real handsomely. You obviously know who I am."

I had been forewarned by the judge that Cioffi would offer the world - or anything else for his freedom.

"I don't think so," I answered. *Can I actually kill an unarmed human being facing me?* I suddenly wondered. "Do you know what happened to your son?" I asked.

"Is that what this's all about?" Cioffi questioned, showing a cold, cynical grin. "I know all about it, and I'm sure we can work things out. Just tell me what you want."

"Tell me what happened to your son," I ordered in a demanding tone.

"He was shot by a guy named Wayne."

"Why?" I asked.

"How the hell do I know?"

"Because there has to be a reason, and I don't think the head of a successful family doesn't have some kind of idea. It won't enhance your cause to lie to me."

Cioffi sat down on the grass and crossed his legs like a grade school kid. "Okay, okay! One of our bookies stiffed us. You can guess what the price is for a double-cross like that in my business."

I nodded. "You find him and break his legs. Or you find him and plan his funeral."

"The latter with this wise cracker."

"What about the girl you kidnapped, and the old man your henchmen beat up?"

"I don't know about any of that silliness. I was still in prison. You know that."

I shook my head. "I told you not to lie to me. I'm sure your men were just following your orders."

"My son's orders."

I smiled, not wide. "Well, I guess he paid for the sins of his father, and now you're going to pay for the sins of your son."

"My life for a million dollars," Cioffi said, his voice almost a cry. He locked his hands in prayer.

"And who pays for your son's death?" I asked.

"The culprit has already paid," Cioffi said. "A fool named Wayne is dead."

I slowly lit a cigarette, dragged deeply and let the smoke slowly escape through my nose. "A so-called fool named Wayne didn't shoot your son."

Cioffi's eyes narrowed. "Well then, who did? I'm not an eye for an eye guy, ya know. I take both eyes."

"I killed him," I said matter-of-factly, and then puffed deeply again - this time blowing one of my famous rings.

Cioffi's eyes widened, his fists clenched. He rose to his feet. "So you kill me before I kill you? Is that it?"

"Some of it. I don't know how many of your sons or how many of your gang served in the Armed Forces in the past few years, but the old man you had beaten risked his life back in 1917. Came home crippled after protecting people like you and me. Your hoods broke into my home and kidnapped an innocent girl who had no way to protect herself. You should be ashamed of yourself - a big man like you."

Cioffi lowered his chin to his chest. "We have a code of honor, pal. Goes back long before me! I guess it is an eye for an eye. You killed my son - so I kill you."

"Oh, yeah?" I blurted. *Can I really kill a man in cold blood?* I asked myself again. *I don't think so.* "Your goons kidnapped my girlfriend and scared the shit out of her. They beat up an old cripple who couldn't defend himself. And after agreeing to let us leave, one of them shot Wayne. What kind of honor is that?"

Cioffi didn't answer right away, maybe weighing the words, how they'd sound, and if he could possibly talk his way out of being executed. "It was the way my father brought me up, and the way I brought my kids up. We're proud of our heritage. Your uncle and the broad were what we call collateral damage."

"I'm sure you're proud," I said, agreeing. "And I know you won't rest 'till you've avenged your son's death. Maybe we can figure out some kind of truce." I quickly recalled that I had no weapon other than the asshole gun in my boot that contained one bullet. I had actually forgotten to bring my regular pistol. *Great hit man I am. Fuck me!* My knife still stuck out from the tree, way too far away to reach. I felt ready to make a deal. I'd just have to put the eight hundred back.

"Hell with you, you little piece of shit." Cioffi's temper had finally got the best of him. From fifteen feet away he rushed at me, flailing his arms.

I froze at the unexpected turn of events. Cioffi was quickly on top of me, knocking us both to the ground, punching and kicking. The man was sixty, but in good shape, and had arms of steel.

I tried to roll over - but failed.

"I pumped iron in the slammer for many years, punk," he said. "Not much else to do in the joint." He grunted as he pounded my head and chest with his flying fists.

This guy's as strong as an ox, I thought to myself, now half conscience. *He's beating me to death.*

With all my remaining strength I brought my knee up into Cioffi's groin.

The Godfather groaned, fell backward, and grabbed his most vulnerable spot. I climbed to my knees, crawled to the tree and pulled the knife out of the bark, turned and aimed at Cioffi's head.

The criminal stood up and smiled. "What are you, some kind of carnival knife thrower? When you miss me, I'll take the knife and cut you up into a hundred ribbons. I don't know who the hell you are or who hired you, but as far as I'm concerned you're a dumb punk who has a stupid uncle and stupid girlfriend. My boys shoulda killed 'em all. And by the way, that'll be the first order I give them. Kill the old fart uncle and your girlfriend - after they've used her a bit, of course. No need to waste supple meat I always say."

Nice man! I sardonically thought as the back of my neck heated up. *Cioffi is actually a father to some boys and brought them up in his image. They respect him! What's this world coming to?*

I stood twenty feet away from my adversary. I stopped talking and took aim as though I was in the Kenmore Hotel barroom trying to flush Pinky Higgins' john. The passing thought brought a smile. Higgins had actually got himself hit with a fastball so I could get my licks at the plate. *Thanks Pinky!* My next shot was for eight hundred dollars - quite a bit more than usual. I flung the knife. It took Cioffi's right ear off. *Damn! Missed again!* The now frightened man's eyes almost popped out of his head. "I thought you wanted a truce," Cioffi said in a pleading tone. "I know when my goose is cooked. I'm sure we can work something out."

I leaned over and pulled Wayne's midget pistol out of my boot. *What would my father have done?* I asked myself, and then recalled my father telling me that: *If you ever find yourself facing a crook and you're carrying a gun, shoot first and tell him to stick 'em up, second. It's safer that way, and you're only twisting the cop code a bit.* He hadn't taken his own advice and paid for it with his life.

I took careful aim. "Stick 'em up," I said in a soft tone, almost inaudible.

Cioffi flashed an incredulous look. "Stick what up, punk?"

I fired! The bullet passed between the surprised man's eyes. He fell forward - dead before he hit the ground.

That's for you, Wayne. Thanks for saving Penny and me.

After burying the body and smoothing over the topsoil on the gravesite I slowly drove back to the city, found an out-of-the-way bar, and soaked myself in dimies. Lots of them! When I arrived at the houseboat I parked the limo and walked down the long pier. It was late, and the combination of fish smell attacking my nostrils along with the beer splashing in my unfed stomach almost made me throw up right in front of two cheaply dressed young women coming out of the houseboat, giggling, and appearing to be counting cash. They barely looked up as they passed me. I thought that I recognized one of them from the Old Howard Burlesque Theater. *Her face?* I wondered. *Maybe! Her tight sweater promising oversized breasts? More likely!* She wore heavy make-up, probably covering an acne condition. *So what? Voyeur attendees of the strip shows aren't interested the girl's faces.*

I half nodded as I passed and entered my home. The Babe and Uncle Bill were sitting in front of the blazing hot wood stove matching shots of vodka and laughing. They were both dressed in their underwear – Bill's long johns with a flap that opened in the seat. It was open! The Babe wore stained white jockey shorts, probably changed weekly whether they needed it or not. *Gross!*

The Babe looked up, smiled and farted. *Gross!*

"Almost caught us having fun," he said and laughed deeply.

I flipped my chauffer cap onto a chair and collapsed onto the couch. "You guys eat yet?"

"An orange," Bill said. "When did you grow that mustache? Looks shitty!"

I had actually forgotten about the disguise, chuckled to myself and addressed The Babe. "I met a girl," I said. "The marrying kind."

"They're all the marrying kind," Babe said. "I tried it twice, but I had the upper hand."

"What's that?"

"Dough! Lots of it."

"I got a new job – if I want to take it. It pays a quite a bit more than being a private dick."

"Bill says you spent two years being a cop. Why didn't you like that job?"

"Too many people telling me what to do. Sometimes I didn't agree, but it never seemed to make any difference."

"So you don't like being bossed around," Uncle Bill said. "What do you think happens in a marriage?"

I walked over to a cabinet containing boxes and cans of food. I grabbed a box of Kellogg's Pep serial and poured myself a bowl. I reached inside the box and pulled out a small pin that depicted a comic character. "Either of you guys have Captain Midnight?"

Bill raised his hand. "I don't have that one. But I don't have a beanie to stick it on either."

I smiled. "I'll buy you one tomorrow."

Babe rubbed his hands together in front of the fire. A cool breeze was filtering in off the harbor. "The world has changed, kid. No more rationing, no more wars - houses that were five thousand before the war are now ten thousand, and new ones are being built in droves. The GIs are getting married and going back to school. The horrible Depression is over. I even bought my wife some nylon stockings last week."

"So what does all that have to do with me settling down and getting married?" I asked.

Bill relit his pipe for the umpteenth time, the smoke seeming to encircle his fedora-covered-dome like a halo. "Have I ever given you a bum steer?" he asked. "Took care of you since you was a kid."

"I know, Bill. And I appreciate all you've done for me. I'm thinking of taking a new job."

"Safer? More dough?" Bill asked.

"No and yes!"

"Do you love the girl?" Babe asked. "Or is she just a good lay?"

I felt a little heat under my collar, but accepted the fact that the two old farts were just trying to help. "I love her now, and let's face it guys, even a bad lay for a guy is a good lay."

Babe and Bill looked at each other and chuckled. "He's learning," Babe said. "He's learning."

"Look son," Bill said while stoking the stove for more heat. "Fifty percent of marriages end in divorce. And probably more than fifty percent of those who try and stick it out don't really like each other. So, where does that leave the sacred institution of marriage?"

I didn't answer.

"And Bill tells me that the girlie lied to you," Babe added. "Is that right?"

"Extenuating circumstances," I snapped.

Bill began humming a pop song of the day, and then added the words, "It was great fun, but it was just one of those things."

"Gimme one of those shot glasses," I said. "Might as well get as drunk as you two fools. Tomorrow is another day."

"And don't forget," Babe said. "You'll always have Kenmore Square."

Just before sun-up the three of us fell into deep sleeps. We had shot darts, played several hands of poker, and verbally solved all the world's problems. My vivid dreams consisted of baseball players dropping fly balls, Penny naked juggling grenades, and several racehorses crossing the finish line in a photo finish at Narragansett Park. Judge Stamos and Mr. Yawkey lectured me on eating three meals a day and getting a good night's sleep. Wayne popped in and out with a big smile on his face. And Rudy York beat on an Indian drum with Uncle Bill's crutches. *Ahh, if only dreams could come true.*

A bright warm late summer sun hung high over Boston Harbor and seeped into the room as I awoke, head aching.

The limo was gone. And so was Babe.

CHAPTER TWENTY-SEVEN

BOSTON POST HEADLINES 1946

DOUGHNUTS NOW PRICED AT 15 CENTS A DOZEN

JUAN PERON ELECTED PRESIDENT OF ARGENTINA

HUGHSON VICTOR OVER INDIANS, 1-0. RED SOX CLINCH ON WILLIAMS INSIDE OF PARK HOMER was the headline in the Boston Globe on September 13, 1946. An article by columnist Burt Whitman read: **Boston's 28 year quest for the World Series became a flaming mathematical certainty today when the Red Sox, on the back of an unprecedented inside-the-park homer by Ted Williams and Tex Hughson's intrepid shutout pitching, beat the Cleveland Indians 1 to 0, while the strangely friendly Yankees were eliminating the second-place Detroit Tigers 5 to 4. As the Red Sox were leading their men in the pennant-clinching celebration tonight, owner Tom Yawkey and manager Joe Cronin made no effort to hide their elation. Yawkey said he always knew Cronin would do it, and Joe gave Yawkey credit for 100 percent cooperation, and then went to town for everybody on the** team. **It was Ted's 38th**

homer of the season, a new high for him. The Sox only managed 2 hits off Cleveland starter Red Embree, and Hughson gave up three.

Later in the week when the team returned home from the winning road trip, the players and sportswriters attended a celebration at the Kenmore Hotel hosted by owner Yawkey. I was invited.

"I don't know how you handled it, Johnny," Mr. Yawkey said to me, now his favorite private detective. "But I haven't heard one word about Majors since you got back from Rhode Island at the end of August with Penny. And you've made yourself mighty scarce. My loyal secretary won't even tell me what happened down there. Was there some kind of connection?"

"Yes and no," I said. "It was a mess. Majors stiffed some bookies. No question that he was hanging with the wrong people. It seemed to everyone involved that the easiest, safest, and sanest path was to allow everything to go away. So that's what we did."

"But, I thought Penny's brother confessed to killing Majors," Yawkey asked, still doubtful. "What was that all about?"

"He recanted his statement when he realized that his sister wasn't a suspect. He originally thought he was protecting her."

Mr. Yawkey put his arm around my shoulder, sipped a straight scotch, and puffed on a big cigar. "Well, my boy, I suppose I shouldn't ask you who did put that little talented prick to rest. But, whatever you did certainly worked out for me and the team - and for Penny too."

Rudy York approached the pair. "You owe my pal a bonus," he addressed the boss.

Mr. Yawkey blinked. "I do? What for? I paid him well for is efforts."

Rudy laughed, sipped on a tall glass of draft beer and said, "Cuz I drove in 118 runs, that's why. You told Johnny that if I drove in over a hundred you'd give him a bonus."

Mr. Yawkey shrugged, reached into his pocket, removed some bills from his wallet and handed them to me.

"I did say that. But the truth is that I can never pay him enough for what he did for me and the team. Penny said he risked his life to save her."

I took a quick glance at the bills before pocketing them. Five one-hundred-dollar-bills. *Thanks Rudy!*

"Thanks, Tom," I said. "That'll buy me a lot of World Series tickets."

"No way!" It was Tex Hughson's voice. "This guy's a good luck charm. Darky sits in the dugout with us, or I don't pitch."

"I second the motion." It was Ted Williams' voice. Ted gave me a friendly punch on the elbow. "Keep that elbow up, kid. A few of us snuck over and watched you play last weekend in the Park League. Not bad! You got three hits. I wish I could hire someone to run for me every time I got on base. By the way, we noticed that you guys had a moment of silence for an old pitcher who I guess had passed away. Pain? Sain?"

"Wayne," I corrected him. "Yeah, he was a good pitcher, hitter, and a good guy. Passed away suddenly. Natural causes! Too bad we don't all have expiration dates on our birth certificates - then we all could plan better." I turned to Mr. Yawkey. "You know what the boss always says to us. It isn't the hand we're dealt, but how we play it."

A reporter butted in and asked Mr. Yawkey some embarrassing questions. "About bigotry, Mr. Yawkey. I guess the Dodgers are going to sign a Negro next year. Any plans for the Red Sox? I understand some of them are pretty good players. Satchel Paige. Josh Gibson."

Mr. Yawkey turned a few shades of red, coughed on his cigar, and curtly answered. "We gave that Robinson guy a tryout last year. He won't amount to anything. And we aren't bigots. We have an Italian playing for us. Dom DiMaggio. We have a Polish kid, Johnny Peskovitch. And we have an Indian."

"Any Jews?" the impetuous reporter asked.

Mr. Yawkey turned his back and walked away in a huff as the reporter smiled and scribbled some notes.

Penny bounced over to the group, smiled at everyone and pulled me away. "I'm borrowing him for a spell, boys. We might not be right back."

They all chuckled and watched Penny drag me into the hallway. "I'm mad at you," she scolded. "You haven't called me for two weeks. And you don't even answer your phone. Did you close your private-eye business? I am in love with you, you know."

I noticed a divan in the corner of the hallway and directed her to it. We sat close, hand in hand. "Sorry," I said. "I've been real busy. I took a security job with Judge Stamos. The pay's good. Too good!"

Penny chugged her drink, eyeing me with hooded eyelids over the top of her glass. "Couldn't you just keep being a private-eye? I thought you did pretty well?"

"I still am! But I kinda owe Wayne."

"Wayne? What does he have to do with the price of eggs?"

"Well, he linked me up with Judge Stamos, and the Judge got your brother out of jail, and you --. Well, it's too hard to explain. Let's just say that everyone lived happily ever after, except, of course, those who died."

Penny frowned and shot me a puzzled look. "I get the feeling that you're giving me the brush off. Is that right, Johnny? Are you brushing me off?"

I rose and pulled Penny to her feet. I wrapped my arms around her and kissed her deeply. I then led her out of the hotel swinging doors into the street and hailed a cab. I handed her a large manila envelope. "The judge says that you and Butch have to leave town, pronto. The Cioffi family is blaming what happened in the restaurant on the Godfather's strange disappearance and want to question you and me. Do you really think that what happened in Rhode Island will go unpunished? There are two plane tickets to Key West in the envelope. Reservations have been made at a small hotel and there is enough money in the envelope to support you and Butch for at least two years - as long as you don't allow your brother to gamble it away. Now please hurry. I do love you, and I promise I'll get in touch once you get settled. Maybe we can date like kids do. You know, I'll visit you and we can go to dinner, dances, and long walks on the beach. What do you say?"

Penny looked perplexed. She wiped a tear from her eye. "If you say so. I'll do it. And I do love you."

Penny climbed into the cab and saluted me as it pulled away from the curb. My paining gut and a freshly bitten cuticle hinted to me that I might never see her again. She had lied to me about Majors and it would take me a long time to come to grips with that fact. Both Murphy and I sincerely thought that she and Butch were one way or another responsible for the killing. Majors deserved it! But allowing her brother to take the rap was questionable. The other stuff about getting married, settling down and having a family? It wasn't debatable. *Hit men don't make good role model fathers,* I decided.

I felt bewitched, bothered, and bewildered as the cab slowly disappeared into the night driving toward Penny's apartment where Murphy and Butch were waiting for her. The plane was scheduled to take off from Logan Airport in two hours. She kept waving out the back window as the cab got smaller and smaller. My chest heaved. My heart ached. *Give, forgive and live,* I recalled her saying to me. *Not so easy,* I thought. I had almost given my life, had given Wayne's instead, not forgiven Penny, and now I had to go on living my own life – maybe a very lonely one.

I then wiped a few tears from my wet eyes. *I guess big boys do cry!*

EPILOGUE

THE RED SOX ENDED THE SEASON with 101 victories, 15 games ahead of the Detroit Tigers. Manager Joe Cronin, never recognized for being an able manager, decided to make the Red Sox play three exhibition games before the World Series started. "Just to keep the boys in sharp shape," he said. The Dodgers and Cardinals had ended the season in a tie - so were forced to play a 2 out of 3 series for the honor of meeting the Sox for all the marbles. Those three extra games kept them in shape and sharp.

During the first unnecessary exhibition game Ted Williams was hit on his right elbow by a pitch and was forced out of the lineup. During the seven game series against the Cardinals he only managed a mere six singles and one RBI. *Thanks Joe!*

The series went to the seventh game, finally won by the Cardinals. Harry Walker drove Enos Slaughter home with the winning run on a double to centerfield. DiMaggio had been hurt in the late innings and came out of the game to be replaced by a mediocre outfielder named Leon Culberson. Slaughter admitted later that he would have never tried to score from first base if DiMaggio had been in the game. *So much for the fates!*

Cronin went on to manage another year, became General Manager, and eventually served as the president of the American League. He died in 1984 at the age of 78 - a Hall of Famer.

A weary Rudy York was traded to Chicago during the middle of the 1947 season, burned up a hotel room with a smoldering cigarette and was almost killed, played a few games with the Phillies in 1948, and then ended up in the minor leagues, slipping all the way to Class D ball. He died broke at age 57 working as a low paid bartender.

Tex Hughson, a 21 game winner in 1946, hurt his arm in 1947, tried to pitch through the pain in 1948 and 1949, and then retired to a ranch in Texas.

Roy Partee became part of a big trade in 1948 that brought Junior Stephens and ace pitcher Jack Kramer to the Red Sox. Partee's career went nowhere after that deal.

Stephens went on to put up great stats for the Red Sox, leading the league in RBIs twice. The Red Sox finished in a tie for 1st place in 1948 only to lose a playoff game to Cleveland who went on to whip the Boston Braves in the World Series.

In 1949 the Sox lost the pennant to the Yankees on the last day of the season.

Pinky Higgins, a favorite drinking buddy of Tom Yawkey, eventually became Red Sox manager, serving two long terms and winning nothing. He was arrested for vehicular homicide and died in prison in 1969 at age 59.

Tom Yawkey owned the team up until he died from leukemia in 1977. His wife Jean took over with the help of rumored boyfriend, the Red Sox second-string catcher, Hayward Sullivan. She subsequently gathered a few minor partners who ended up disagreeing. The team finally went into a Yawkey Trust Foundation with trust attorney, John Harrington taking over control.

In the summer of 1991, at Cooperstown, New York, the home of Baseball's Hall of Fame museum, Harrington played in a fun doubles tennis match. His partner was the late John Henry Williams (Ted Williams son, an excellent tennis player and not such a good baseball player). The opponents were the author of this book and the then National League president, former St. Louis Cardinal All Star first baseman Bill White. No official results are admitted by the author other than that White, Harrington and Williams were very good players. White recently wrote a book about his ultra interesting baseball life called Uppity. Google it! You'll like it! He played for 13 years, radio and TV announced for the Yankees with Phil Rizzuto for 17 years, and then served as president of the National League for 5 years. Sounds like a Hall of Fame spot in Cooperstown should be found for him. Dontcha think?

Harrington sold the Red Sox in 2001 for over 600 million dollars.

Documents reveal that Harry Frazee (the man who sold Babe Ruth to the Yankees in 1920) bought the team in 1915 for a little over $600,000. Inflation?

The Red Sox finally got their revenge against St. Louis in the 2004 World Series sweeping them four games to none.

Ronald Nash did flee to Key West in 1946, had his face and name changed, spent a year in hiding, moved to the Miami area and became a race track jockey's agent handling some successful thoroughbred race riders.

Detective Murphy became Boston Police Chief and retired in 1960, living handsomely on a nice pension until his death in 1981.

Uncle Bill Dark lived on the houseboat in Boston Harbor until his death at age 85 in 1967.

Penny Mitchell never returned to Boston and neither did her brother.

Johnny Dark? He did attend the 1946 World Series, sitting in the dugout with his ex-teammates. And he did work with Judge Stamos for the next twenty years. When the judge died, the former P.I. retired and headed south in search for his never forgotten shell part. And he would have enjoyed reporting that he found her and that they lived happily ever after. But that never happened.

Dark currently lives very close to the old houseboat location in a nice high-rise condo on Atlantic Avenue. He's a semi-healthy, ninety plus year old who stays in shape by walking the local beaches picking up interesting seashells.

Did the Red Sox have a pitcher named Steve Majors attend Spring Training in 1946? You could ask Penny or Butch Michaels if you could find them.

And if you could find Jonathan Dark, up until now he'd deny it. But you will find him listed in the Boston telephone book white pages if you feel like looking. But, on the other hand, maybe he has a cell phone and isn't listed.

Bobby Doerr and Dave Ferris, All-Stars from the 1946 team are still alive (2012). Johnny Pesky passed away in August 2012. Pesky and Doerr attended the April 100th Anniversary Tribute Day and were questioned by this author, neither admitting anything. But, come to think of it, neither denied it. Hmm! They supposedly swore to secrecy in 1946. Remember the memo Mr. Yawkey posted for the team in the beginning of this chronicle?

And everyone knows the old cliché - if you tell a lie enough times you begin believe it.

And does Dark's record of one hit in one time at bat equaling a batting average of one thousand still appear in the record books? Look it up in the Official Baseball Encyclopedia. That information (maybe), and most definitely all of the other stats that appear in this book are recorded there. Scouts Honor!

But wait one cotton pickin' minute. Here's something that slipped through the cracks, and it might change your mind about what really happened that dreary August evening back in the summer of 1946 – and why.

EXTRA CHAPTER

AS THE LATE FALL SUN SET OVER BOSTON HARBOR I locked the houseboat door real good as I continued trying to put everything behind me and move forward one day at a time. Penny and Butch had been gone for two months and I hadn't called her. *Should I call Penny?* I kept asking myself. I didn't know.

The Babe had gone back south to play golf, and only a still recuperating Uncle Bill was left as a reminder. Sadly, the Babe had slowed down a lot, still smoking, drinking, eating and whoring – but his spirit had waned – and he coughed too much. I wondered if it meant anything bad. I thought of a saying that my father used to quote: *A candle that burns twice as strong, lives half as long.* The Babe burned every candle he could find.

I poured myself a scotch with ice and checked Bill's room to make sure he hadn't barhopped and got lost. He was sound asleep.

Good!

The phone rang.

I answered.

It was Murphy.

"Got some interesting information for you," he said. "Might clear up some stuff, but might really muddy the waters."

"Shoot," I said. "Nothing can mess up my life any more than it is right now."

"Don't bet on it," Murphy said. "It took awhile, but I got the final autopsy on Majors."

I sat up with a jerky motion. "Are you kidding? What the hell took so long, and who the hell cares?"

"That's the point. No one cares, and that's why it took so long. We thought we knew what happened - so buried the investigation and the corpse in a pauper's grave. That's another reason why it was never in the newspapers. No one even cared or knew the guy existed."

I sank back in the soft cushions of my sofa. I could almost smell the remnants of Penny's perfume – but no, she hadn't been in the houseboat for two months.

"The tide didn't kill him," Murphy said. "He had a broken rib cage. Someone squeezed him real tight. We figure they then tied him where we found him hoping he'd drown when the tide came in. But, it didn't happen that way. By the time the water table rose over the poor guy's head, he was already dead."

I downed the whole tall glass of scotch, felt it burn my esophagus making me choke. "Butchy?"

"Not really! At least I don't think so. Not strong enough. Remember, Majors was a big boy. And it's for damn sure your girlfriend didn't do it. It was done by someone physically powerful."

I felt a choke and muttered. "That means that my brilliant deductions were all wrong. Poor Penny was totally innocent all along. She didn't plan it. She didn't' sanction it. She didn't even know about it. Fuck me! What a fool I've been."

Murphy muttered back. "Ditto! You erase all that blackboard yet, and clap those erasers?"

I lifted my tired head. The room was quite dim, but I could make out some very hazy chalk words still on the wall blackboard. "No! I think some of it is still there. Why do you ask?"

"You know how to play the game. Check the names that are left. We're headin' home on this one, pal."

I walked to the wall, rubbed my eyes and studied. All the ballplayers had been erased. Nash had been erased. Wilson had been erased. Butch hadn't been erased. Penny's name had never been written. Only one name remained - the most recent addition. Bull Brown - the wrestler.

"Bull Brown," I exclaimed. "Broken ribs you say? Hey, maybe he was jealous. Yeah! What do you think?"

"We think he did it. Pinned for the count of three! We already picked him up. He has a record a mile long – petty theft, assault – no killings yet. He's got a sleazy lawyer who got him out on bail. And he's got a shitty alibi that'll probably stick. I don't think we'll get any other evidence other than he was in love with Charlie Wilson, who, by the way, has disappeared. But, I'm telling ya, if you had witnessed the questioning – well, I'm sure you'd of known he did it. He didn't volunteer anything – and you know what that's supposed to mean."

"So you're convinced?"

"I'd stake my badge on it, and I'd throw in a weekend of pinch running for you in the Park League."

I hung up!

A week later a front-page story in the daily Boston Post ran an article:

LOCAL PROFESSIONAL WRESTLER FOUND DROWNED IN THE CHARLES RIVER. FOUL PLAY SUSPECTED. BULL BROWN, 34, SOUTH BOSTON BORN, WHO LAST SUMMER FOUGHT CHAMPION STEVE CRUSHER CASEY AND LOST, WAS FOUND LATE LAST NIGHT FLOATING FACE DOWN NEAR THE HARVARD BOAT HOUSE ON THE CAMBRIDGE SIDE OF THE RIVER. A NINE-INCH KNIFE WOUND WAS DETECTED IN HIS THROAT. POLICE HAVE NO SUSPECTS.

Made in the USA
Charleston, SC
19 September 2013